THE
SECRET
GARDEN

THE CINEMATIC NOVEL

THE
SECRET
GARDEN

THE CINEMATIC NOVEL

Adapted by
LINDA CHAPMAN

Based on the screenplay by
JACK THORNE

Based on the original novel by
FRANCES HODGSON BURNETT

HARPER
An Imprint of HarperCollinsPublishers

Library of Congress Control Number: 2019956227

ISBN 978-0-06-297102-9

20 21 22 23 24   PC/LSCH   10 9 8 7 6 5 4 3 2

❖

Originally published in Great Britain by HarperCollins Publishers, 2020

THE
SECRET
GARDEN

THE CINEMATIC NOVEL

1

Noises in the Night

Mary Lennox couldn't sleep. A large ceiling fan spun slowly around and around, but it was too warm to get comfortable. Outside, in the dark Indian night, the sounds of insects chirping were drowned out by people shouting. *The servants are being very noisy tonight,* Mary thought. *Why doesn't Daddy tell them to be quiet?* Sitting up in bed, she pushed her chin-length hair back behind her ears and picked up her rag doll.

"Jemima, can you sleep?" she whispered. Jemima stared back at her.

Mary liked to pretend that Jemima could understand everything she said because talking to Jemima and telling her stories helped Mary feel less lonely and bored. She didn't have any brothers or sisters, and the servants—apart from her ayah, her Indian nanny—kept their distance. Mary wasn't allowed to play outside much because the sun was very strong. Her father was too busy with his work to play games with her as much as she'd like and her mother . . . Mary chewed her lower lip. She knew her mother didn't like her. At times, Mary even suspected that she hated her.

Well, I hate her too, Mary thought, scowling.

There was a scream from somewhere in the villa and then the sound of a crash and a door slamming. A wisp of fear curled in Mary's tummy as she glanced at her bedroom door. What was going on?

She'd heard her father talking to his friends about how there was a lot of fighting in India at the moment. Mary didn't really understand, but it sounded like the Indian people didn't want the English to be in India anymore and wanted them to leave. Daddy and his friends had talked about fighting in the streets. But surely those streets were a long way away, in distant cities. The Indian servants who worked for the Lennox family did whatever they were told, so Mary couldn't imagine them fighting. No, she was safe here. Nothing bad would happen to her.

Trying not to listen to the muffled bangs and crashes and shouts from outside her room, she stroked Jemima's woolen hair. "Are you scared, Jemima?" she whispered. "Well, don't be. It's just grown-ups being grown-ups. Shall I tell you a story to make you feel better?"

Lighting a lantern, she got out of bed and took Jemima to a den she had made out of cushions and throws in the middle of her room. She began to recite one of her favorite stories, using shadow puppets to act it out as she spoke. It was a story her ayah had told her about a boy named Rama and a girl named Sita who loved each other, but then, one day, a demon kidnapped Sita and took her away. Ayah's stories were always filled with gods and demons, magic and excitement.

By the time Mary was nearing the end, the noises outside had quieted down, and her eyelids were starting to feel heavy. "Rama was just about to catch up with Sita and the demon, but then the demon threw down fire and imprisoned him in flames," she said, yawning. "Luckily, the fire god, Agni, was watching and he parted the flames and carried Rama up into the clouds. After that, the two of them set off, looking—ever looking—for Rama's love," she finished.

Blowing out the lantern, Mary sank back on the cushions with Jemima in her arms. Her eyelashes fluttered, and a few seconds later she was asleep.

A damp green lawn . . . flower beds filled with pink, lilac, and blue flowers . . . trees with branches bursting with blossom . . . Mary ran down a path past statues. . . . A grown-up was holding her hand. She was laughing, trying not to fall over, and she felt happy, wonderfully and completely happy. . . .

Slowly, Mary began to wake up. For a moment, she tried to hold on to the familiar dream, but it faded just like it always did. The dream garden looked so different from any garden she had ever known, but it seemed so real to her when she was there and she always felt truly happy in it. With a sigh, she rubbed her eyes. The first thing she noticed was that the shutters were still open and it was very bright outside. Sunlight was flooding in through the window. Mary's tummy rumbled. Where was her ayah? Why hadn't she brought her breakfast?

Feeling hungry and cranky, she sat up in her den. "Ayah!" she called loudly. To her surprise, the door didn't open to reveal her ayah's kindly face. Feeling even crankier, Mary raised her voice. "Ayah! I'm calling you! It's late and I'm not even dressed!" Her voice reached shouting pitch. *"AYAH!"*

Mary waited. Still no one came. What was going on? The house was very quiet. That was peculiar, she realized. Usually, she could hear the servants bustling around. Unease flickered through her as she remembered the strange noises in the night.

"Should . . . should we go and look around and see if we can find anyone, Jemima?" She tried to sound brave, but her voice trembled slightly. "Yes, I think that's a very good idea," she went on. "Don't worry. I'll look after you. We'll go and find Daddy, and he shall get Ayah for us."

Opening the door of her bedroom, she paused. The corridor outside her room was in chaos. Pictures had been pulled from the walls and were now lying on the floor without their gold frames. Heart beating fast, Mary started to hurry through the villa. Every room was the same—curtains had been torn down, ornaments lay smashed on the floor, much of the furniture had disappeared, and in the kitchen, the cupboards were open and the shelves bare. Everything of any value had vanished, and worst of all, there was no one there at all.

"Father? Daddy? Ayah?" Mary's voice rose anxiously. She pushed the doors to the veranda open. The sun shone down brightly, but the garden was as deserted as the house. Mary clutched Jemima.

"Where have they all gone?" she whispered.

2

A Long Journey

Mary sat on a wooden bench on the deck of an enormous ship as it chugged across the vast ocean, leaving India and heading toward England. Her back was straight, and she stared silently up at the sky, holding Jemima in her arms. Nearby, a group of children was playing noisily on the deck, but Mary didn't join in with them. It had been several weeks since she had woken up and found her home had been ransacked, but it felt like a lifetime ago.

No one had come to the house for two days, until two English officers turned up. They had been astonished to find her there—dirty, thirsty, hungry—and had taken her to the hospital. She had asked them where her father and mother were, but they had just told her to be a good girl and not to worry. At the hospital, a nurse gave her something to eat and drink, and had helped Mary bathe and change into clean clothes. Then Mary was seen by a doctor. Neither the nurse nor the doctor would answer her questions about her parents either.

As she waited in a small room, wondering when Daddy was going to come and take her home and what he would say when he found out that all the servants had vanished, she heard the two officers talking in a room next door.

"This is a frightful mess," said one gravely. "Poor

child. If only we had evacuated the family before the trouble broke out. The cholera epidemic couldn't have come at a worse time for them."

Mary pricked her ears. She knew that cholera was a disease that killed lots of people, but what did it have to do with her family?

"The doctor tells me her mother was struck down with cholera very suddenly. Her father rushed her here in the night, but it was too late," the first officer continued.

Mary froze, foreboding running down her spine. Too late for what?

"The mother died that night and then the father died the next morning."

Mary's heart started to pound so fast she thought it was going to burst out of her chest. *Mother and Daddy . . . both dead?* She drew in a sharp breath. No, they couldn't be dead. They couldn't be! But even as the thought formed she knew, with a horrible, crashing certainty, that it must be true. The officers wouldn't make a mistake about something like that. A sob ripped up through her, half whimper, half choking cry.

There was the sound of feet, and one of the officers looked in through the door. "Oh, Lord. She's here." He cleared his throat awkwardly, obviously having no idea how to comfort a ten-year-old girl.

His companion joined him. "What in heaven's name are we going to do with her? She can't stay here," he said.

Mary looked up through her tears to see the first officer consulting his notes.

"She has a widowed uncle in England," he said. "We'll send her back on the boat with the other children."

From then on, Mary was passed around like an unwanted parcel. On leaving the hospital, she was sent to stay with a clergyman named Mr. Crawford, who had a wife and five children of his own. She heard the adults around her saying it would be better for her to be with other children, but she didn't understand why. She didn't want to play with the Crawford children. They were younger than her, and they wanted to know all about her parents and how they had died. She felt miserable and wouldn't answer their questions. Finally, she lost her temper, ripping up a drawing that the youngest had done for her and screaming at them all to leave her alone. After that, they stayed away from her, watching her as if she was a strange, wild animal. Mary didn't care. She didn't feel like she would care about anything ever again.

She had heard the clergyman and his stout, well-meaning wife talking about her in whispers: "Poor child . . . word has been sent to England . . . He's her uncle by marriage, you know. . . . He was married to her mother's twin sister, who died years ago. . . . Such a tragedy, poor man . . . but he's her only living relative. . . . He'll have to take her, whether he likes it or not. . . ."

Finally, a telegram had arrived. "The ship that will take you to England leaves tomorrow," Mrs. Crawford informed Mary. "Your uncle—Mr. Craven—who was married to your aunt, Grace, has agreed to take you in. He lives in Yorkshire at a place called Misselthwaite Manor. You're a lucky girl, Mary. Your uncle is a rich man."

Mary swallowed. How could Mrs. Crawford possibly say she was lucky? Her parents were dead, and she was going to live with some old uncle in a horrible house in a strange country! Tears pricked her eyes, but she wouldn't cry in front of the Crawfords—she wouldn't!

Pressing her lips tightly together, she nodded and then walked up the stairs. Reaching her bedroom, she shut the door behind her and then threw herself down on the bed, sobbing into the pillow to muffle her bitter tears.

The ship that carried Mary from Bombay to England was crowded and noisy. There were many families on board, all returning to England because of the unrest in India. Mary had to eat with the other children and do what she was told. She hated it—the food was horrible and the other children were rough and loud. On the first day, she had pushed her plate of food away. "This is disgusting!" she said.

A scruffy boy sitting next to her grabbed her plate and emptied the food onto his own plate.

Mary stared at him, outraged. "I didn't say you could do that!"

"You didn't say I couldn't," the boy replied. "If you aren't going to eat it, I am."

"You don't understand," Mary exclaimed. "I need better food than this. My parents are dead."

He shrugged. "We've all lost, girl."

Mary watched as he gobbled up her food. She didn't like him much, but he was the only person who had spoken to her so far. "Would . . . would you like to hear a story?" she asked tentatively.

He gave her a scornful look. "No, I'm not a child." He got up and moved away to sit by someone else, leaving Mary on her own. Since then, she had barely spoken a word to anyone.

Standing up, Mary now walked to the side of the ship. A railing ran around the deck, and the deep blue ocean swelled below. She lifted up Jemima. Maybe she could tell her one of Ayah's tales and escape into it, forgetting everything else. Telling stories had always been her way of coping when Mother didn't want to see her or when Daddy was too busy to play.

"I'll tell you a story, Jemima," she said. "Just like I used to do at home. There once was a lord of the seas. His name was Varuna and he . . . and he . . ."

The words seemed to dry up in her head. She tried again. "Varuna was very powerful. He . . ." She faltered. But it was no use. All Mary could think about was home.

"I don't have a home, do I, Jemima?" she whispered. "I don't belong anywhere or to anyone now."

Mary felt a sudden stab of pain as she looked into Jemima's blank face. Jemima was just a doll, not a friend. Only children played with dolls, and children had to eat what they were given and keep quiet. Children were passed from place to place; children had to do what grown-ups wanted. She suddenly made up her mind.

"I'm not a child," she said fiercely. "Not anymore."

She let Jemima go. As the doll hit the water far below, shock filled Mary. What had she just done? Jemima floated on the surface for a moment. She stared up at Mary one last time, and then the waves dragged her under.

A lump swelled painfully in Mary's throat, but she swallowed it back. *No more tears,* she told herself. She lifted her chin, her eyes defiant. She wasn't going to cry again—not now, not ever.

Crossing her arms, she turned away from the railings, a lock snapping shut on her broken heart.

3

Misselthwaite Manor

When the ship arrived in England, Mary was met by a stern-looking woman with gray hair. She wore a buttoned-up blue woolen overcoat, with just the hint of a scarf at the neck, and had a leather handbag over her arm. She looked Mary up and down, and from the way her forehead crinkled, Mary had a feeling she didn't approve of what she saw. "My name is Mrs. Medlock," she announced. "I am Mr. Craven's housekeeper, and you are to come with me."

Mary was reminded of a word her father had once used to describe the elderly aunt of a colleague. *Formidable,* he had called her. *Yes, formidable is just what Mrs. Medlock is,* thought Mary. But she reminded herself that Mrs. Medlock was just the housekeeper—a servant—and so had to do what the family told her to do.

Remembering her decision not to be a child anymore, Mary met Mrs. Medlock's gaze. "Very well," she said coldly.

Head held high, Mary followed Mrs. Medlock to the train that was to take them to Yorkshire. As the whistle went and the train started to puff along the rails, clouds of steam shooting out from its funnel, Mary became aware that Mrs. Medlock was studying her.

"Well, you're a plain little piece of goods, aren't

you?" Mrs. Medlock said in her Yorkshire accent.

Mary puzzled over the words, trying to work out what they meant. *I think it's her way of saying I'm not very pretty,* she decided. Mary didn't mind the comment because she didn't consider herself particularly pretty either. She didn't have the long golden hair of a princess in a storybook or the jet-black hair and enchanting brown eyes of the Indian girls in her ayah's tales. She was small and skinny with hair the color of a chestnut. Her skin was pale, her inquisitive hazel eyes almost too large for her face. *Her words are true,* Mary thought, *but what a strange thing for a servant to say.*

She turned and stared out of the window.

Opposite her, Mrs. Medlock settled herself more firmly in her seat. "Now I don't know what you've been told, girl," she began with a warning note in her voice, "but don't be expecting luxury at Misselthwaite. It's not the house it was."

Mrs. Medlock's eyes grew distant, and for a moment Mary had a feeling she was reliving the past.

"When the young mistress was alive, there was a full household staff, a stable of horses, grand balls, but that's all changed now." She tutted indignantly. "Those army savages! They turned the house into a hospital during the war. Brought the wounded, the dead, and the dying. They set up camp in the garden and kept their sick in the ballroom. Quite took over the place, and now there's no knowing what to do with the house. They left it a wreck!"

Mary didn't say anything.

Mrs. Medlock clearly expected more of a response. "Well? Don't you even care?"

"Does it matter whether I care or not?" said Mary bluntly.

Mrs. Medlock's eyes narrowed. She gazed at her for a long moment. "Well, you are an odd duck, aren't you?"

Mary's initial dislike of the housekeeper intensified, and she turned to look out of the window again, not wanting to talk to her anymore. Mrs. Medlock sniffed and got out a book to read.

As the train headed north, Mary continued to gaze out. England was so gray! Rain slanted against the train window. Sodden fields stretched in all directions, cows and sheep hanging their heads in the downpour. It was so different from the bright sunshine of India. There the rain was as welcomed as a longed-for guest, making flowers burst into life and fresh green buds push their way up through the parched soil.

On and on the train went, until they pulled into a station and transferred to a car driven by an unsmiling, gruff man. As they drove away from the station, Mary fell asleep. When she woke up, she saw an endless expanse of gray on either side of the car. She had never seen anything like it. "Is that the sea?" she asked as she looked at the clouds swirling across the top.

"The sea! What a foolish thing to say, girl. Out there are the moors," snorted Mrs. Medlock. "Be sure to stay inside when the mist is rolling or you may not find your way home."

From her tone of voice, it sounded as if she didn't think that would be a bad thing. Mary's lips tightened. She had the strong feeling that Mrs. Medlock didn't want her at Misselthwaite any more than she wanted to be there. *Well, she can stay out of my way and I'll stay out of hers,* she thought fiercely. *All I want is to be left alone.*

They drove on and on along the narrow strip of road that cut across the moors, past heather, sheep, and wild ponies. Occasionally, through the shroud of mist, Mary thought she saw the glow of orange and red flames flickering weakly, and once, she was sure she caught sight of a group of raggedly dressed people trudging beside a pony and cart, but as she looked more closely, the mist closed in and the shadowy figures vanished from sight.

It seemed as if the journey would never end, but finally they turned down a long drive. Parkland stretched away on either side until it merged with the moors. At the end of the drive was an enormous stone manor house with sharp turrets silhouetted against the twilight sky. A single weak light shone out of an upstairs window.

"There it is," Mrs. Medlock announced with a touch of pride in her voice as she looked at the dark, forbidding fortress of a house. "Misselthwaite."

As the car swept through the gates, Mary noticed a robin perched on one of the pillars. For a moment, it seemed to look straight at Mary, and then it flew away.

The car stopped. Mary gazed up at the vast

house and felt a shiver run through her. It looked like the kind of place where ghosts and phantoms walked at night.

"This is your home now," said Mrs. Medlock. "Thanks to your uncle's kindness." She fixed Mary with a stern look. "Now, when you see him, you're not to stare, girl. Do you understand?"

Mary was puzzled. Why ever did Mrs. Medlock think she would stare at her uncle?

Mrs. Medlock went on. "He's suffered enough, poor man. And now to see you, looking the way you do . . . No." She shook her head as if that would be too much. "A shadow, that's what you'll have to be at Misselthwaite, girl. Just a shadow."

Mary had no idea why the way she looked might upset her uncle, but before she could ask, Mrs. Medlock was already leading the way up the stone steps to the iron-bound oak front door. Mary followed her into the huge entrance hall. Portraits of stern-looking ladies and men frowned down from the walls, and a wide central staircase led up to a landing with a huge window. It couldn't have been more unlike the bright, airy villa where she had lived in India.

"First things first," said Mrs. Medlock, marching over to a brass light switch on the wall. "We're fully electric." She pulled the switch down. The huge glass chandelier in the center of the hall lit up briefly, but then there was a fizzling sound and the lights went out again. Mrs. Medlock raised her eyebrows. "But that doesn't mean it always works. So, if you're needing the facilities in the night, take a lamp. Second, the master is a widower and on his own. He has promised you will have someone to look after you soon enough, but in the meantime don't you be expecting there'll be people to talk to you because there won't."

Standing in the cavernous hall, Mary refused

to be daunted. She lifted her chin. "I need no entertaining. I am not a child."

She felt a stab of satisfaction as she saw the housekeeper blink in surprise. Mrs. Medlock turned and led the way up the grand staircase. On the first landing the staircase split, heading off in opposite directions. Mary followed her down a long, gloomy corridor.

"This house is six hundred years old," said Mrs. Medlock as the corridor twisted and turned past endless closed doors. "There are near a hundred rooms. You'll be told which ones you can go into and those you're to keep out of, but until then you're to stick to your rooms and your rooms only. Is that understood?" Mary nodded. "You may play in the grounds outside, but no exploring the house." Mrs. Medlock gave her a warning look. "No poking about."

Mary met her gaze. "I assure you, Mrs. Medlock,

that I have no interest in 'poking about.'"

"Hmm," Mrs. Medlock sniffed and stopped beside a door. "This is you," she said, opening a door to a bedroom. Mary went inside, and Mrs. Medlock quickly shut the door behind her. She heard the housekeeper walking away, her boots tapping on the floorboards.

Looking around the vast room, Mary felt very small. There was an iron bed with a thin cover and one thin pillow. Next to it was a bedside cabinet with a single lamp. The floor was just bare wooden boards with a couple of threadbare rugs, and the walls were covered with fading wallpaper painted with trees and birds. There was a huge window with long, heavy curtains on either side, a small fire burning in the grate, and an old rocking horse and a battered toy chest.

So this is my new bedroom, Mary thought, looking around at the shabby, old-fashioned things. *No, I will not cry,* she thought fiercely as she felt her throat tighten. She wondered about her uncle. She had thought she would be introduced to him when she arrived, but maybe he didn't want to see her. Mrs. Medlock's words had certainly given her the impression that he hadn't wanted her to come to Misselthwaite.

No one wants me, she thought, her heart swelling with a desperate loneliness. *No one likes me. Everyone probably wishes I had died in India.*

She took off her boots and coat and got under the thin embroidered coverlet of the bed, drawing her knees up to her chest. She thought of India—the sunshine, the bright red and yellow orchids that bloomed after the rain, the monkeys in the trees, the ripe mangoes; Daddy swinging her around in his arms and calling her his little monkey; her ayah smiling fondly at her, happy to bring the little *Miss Sahib* whatever she wanted.

I want to go back, Mary thought longingly. *To my home, to the sunshine and the flowers. I want to wake up and see Daddy and Ayah and for this all to be a terrible nightmare.*

A little voice piped up inside her. *But it isn't a nightmare. It's real, and it all happened because of the wish you made. . . .*

No! She didn't want to think about that.

Staring hard at the embroidered flowers on the coverlet, Mary made herself imagine they were real flowers, vibrant and sweet-smelling. As her imagination began to work its magic, they seemed to brighten and grow in front of her eyes, moving, bending, sweeping her far, far away. . . .

Mary was back in her garden in India. It was part dream, part memory from a year ago. She ran toward the palm tree, her legs pounding. She'd climbed it the day before. For the first time, she'd got up it by herself, and now she wanted her mother to see. She wanted her to be proud of her! Glancing back at the villa, she saw her mother walking along the veranda, one hand on her forehead, her head bowed.

"Mother! Look, I'm climbing!" Mary shouted, starting to climb up. Higher and higher she went. "Mother? Look, please!" Her voice rose as she glanced around, hoping her mother had seen her triumphant climb. But her mother was walking back into the house. She hadn't even glanced in Mary's direction. . . .

Mary woke up in the dark, feeling unhappy and cold. Her eyes darted around. Where was she? As she spotted the shadowy rocking horse and the enormous stone window, it all came back to her. Of course. She was at Misselthwaite Manor. Some-one had been into her room, taken away her coat and boots, and shut the curtains while she'd been asleep—Mrs. Medlock maybe or a maid?

Mary shivered, wanting more blankets. In India she had always had a bell by her bed, and whenever she had rung it, her ayah had appeared. But here there was no bell. "Hello?" she tried calling. She raised her voice. "Hello?" But her words just rang out in the eerie silence.

A high wail from somewhere in the house made her jump. It sounded like a child, but there were no other children here in the manor house. Was it a bird or an animal maybe? Mary heard the noise again. Swinging her legs out of bed, she padded inquisitively to the bedroom door. The sound seemed to be coming from a floor above the one she was on. Perhaps it was her uncle. She listened, head to one side. It didn't sound like a grown man. A worrying thought struck her. *Could . . . could it be a ghost?*

A shiver passed over her skin and for a moment Mary wondered if she should just stay in her room and ignore it. But her curiosity got the better of her. She had to find out what was making such a dreadful noise.

Gathering her courage, she left her room and set off along the gloomy corridor.

4

The House at Night

Mary reached a spiral staircase that looked as if it was a way for servants to move between floors. The sound still seemed to be coming from above her. As she started up the steps, the cries stopped. "Hello? Is someone there?" she called softly.

No one replied, and so she continued up the dark, twisty staircase. The wails started again and then stopped. Quickening her pace, Mary reached a landing lit by a shaft of moonlight filtering in through a window at the end. She hurried along the dark, narrow corridor and turned the corner.

There was a ghost! Mary stopped with a gasp as she saw a girl standing at the far end of the corridor. It took her a few seconds to realize that she was looking at an enormous mirror and the phantom girl was just her own reflection. She let out a relieved breath and felt her racing heart start to slow down.

There was a sudden noisy clatter overhead, and Mary's nerve failed her. Turning, she sprinted back along the corridor as if a whole army of phantoms were after her. She dived into her bedroom and slammed the door shut, leaning against it and gasping for breath. As her breathing calmed, she hurried to her bed, pulled the coverlet over her head, and shut her eyes. She didn't open them again until morning.

When Mary woke next, she saw that light was shining around the edges of the heavy curtains. Had her nighttime adventure really happened?

She got out of bed, pulled open the curtains, and saw that her room looked out onto the sweeping driveway and, beyond the driveway, out onto the misty moors. As Mary watched, a man came out of the house, dragging an old iron bedframe behind him. He flung it onto the gravel. He was about as old as her father and was wearing dark trousers and a waistcoat over a shirt with rolled-up sleeves. His face was craggy and sad, etched with deep wrinkles, and his hair was messy.

That must be my uncle, Mary thought.

There was something odd about him. It was his back, she realized. He had a hump on his shoulders that made him bend over slightly at the waist. Mrs. Medlock's strange words—*you're not to stare, girl*—suddenly made sense. Mary peered down with interest, wondering why no one had ever told her that her uncle was a hunchback. She wouldn't have minded. She had once read a story about a man with a crooked back who had married a beautiful princess whom he had loved very much.

He hurried back into the house and reappeared a minute later, dragging another bed. This time Mrs. Medlock was with him.

"Sir!" she exclaimed. "Please leave the beds. The army will come and collect them. You don't need to do this."

"It needs sorting out," he said stubbornly.

"I know but not like this. You'll do yourself an injury. Please, sir, come back inside." Mrs. Medlock gave him a pleading look. Mary saw her uncle run a hand through his hair and then give in. As he started to follow Mrs. Medlock back into the house, he glanced up toward Mary's window. Mary ducked down, not wanting him to see she had been spying on him. She retreated back into her room, thinking about the lines etched in her uncle's face. He wasn't very old, but he looked like someone who had suffered.

Just then, the bedroom door opened and a maid came in. She was neatly dressed in a gray dress buttoned up to the neck and looked about twenty. Her thick dark hair was tied back tidily in a low bun, and she was carrying a tray with a bowl of porridge on it.

Mary wondered why the maid hadn't knocked before entering. "Who are you?"

"What's that for a greeting?" said the maid with a smile.

Mary blinked at her impudence.

"You'll call me Martha. You're Mary, I hear,"

the maid went on. After putting the tray down, she went over to the fireplace.

Mary stared at her. She was used to Indian servants who never spoke unless they were spoken to. They would answer her if she asked a question, but otherwise they bowed and stayed silent.

Martha began to rake out the cinders. "There's a fine chill in the air today, isn't there?" she went on chattily as she spread paper on top of the ash. "But spring is on its way. That's what my brother, Dickon, says. He's always out on the moors and knows more about nature and animals than anyone."

Mary frowned. She wasn't sure she liked this talkative servant. "I was cold in the night," she said accusingly. "No one heard when I called."

"I'm guessing that's because we were all in our beds too," the maid said. "There's a second blanket under your bed if you're cold tonight."

"And I heard noises too," Mary went on. "Wailing, screaming."

"No," Martha said firmly, adding a layer of coal to the fire. "You heard the wind, that's all. It blows right bad around the house."

Mary considered this. Maybe Martha was right and she'd gotten scared over nothing. Not wanting to seem foolish, she changed the subject.

"Well, I needed someone. You should sleep outside my room. My ayah did, and she would always come if I called her."

To her astonishment, Martha just raised her eyebrows. "Well, whoever Ayah is, she's sure as not here, is she?" she said, lighting the fire. "And I won't be sleeping outside your room tonight or any other night. I'll be sleeping in my own bed, thank you very much."

"But aren't you going to be my servant?" said Mary, surprised.

"Your servant?" Martha's smile widened. "No, girl. I'm just here to check the fire's lit, the room's shipshape, and you've food in you. Nothing more. I've got countless other jobs to do around the house. Now eat your porridge. It's getting cold."

Mary inspected the porridge. It was lumpy and had a skin forming on top of it. She didn't like the look of it at all. "I don't eat porridge," she informed Martha, lifting her chin. "For my breakfast, I like bacon and eggs." She waited for Martha to take the tray away and fetch her something else, but Martha just grinned.

"I like them too but you've got porridge. Now come on, time to get yourself dressed," Martha said, opening the wardrobe. Mary saw it was filled with clothes for her. Martha handed her a dress, some undergarments, stockings, and a cardigan.

"You want me to dress myself?" said Mary, astounded. "But aren't you going to do that?" Her ayah had always dressed her.

"Dress you?" echoed Martha. "Whatever for? You've got hands and arms, haven't you?" She shook her head. "Goodness, Mother always said she couldn't see why grand people's children didn't turn out to be fools. What with needing help with washing and dressing and being took out to walk as if they were puppies." She chuckled. "I see what she means now."

Mary's temper snapped. How dare this rude maid laugh at her! With an angry exclamation, she stamped her foot, her fists scrunching up at her sides.

Martha took a startled step backward. For a moment, there was a long pause, then she shook her head. "And to think I was excited to have a young 'un in the house," she said ruefully as she turned and left the room.

Mary stared after her. Martha had seemed hurt.

I don't understand, Mary thought. She rubbed her forehead. Things were so different in England.

She looked at the clothes in her arms. If children dressed themselves in England, then that's what she would do. She certainly didn't want to give that maid a chance to laugh at her anymore. Chin jutting with determination, Mary managed to get dressed, pulled on the vest and undergarments and the woolen stockings. Then she put the dress over the top. It was an old-fashioned pinafore style, loose-fitting with long sleeves and a hem that reached her knees, but Mary didn't care. Clothes were clothes, and at least this dress was easy to put on.

When she was dressed, she took a few mouthfuls of porridge. It was cold and lumpy now, and she began to wish she'd eaten some of it when it was still warm. She looked around the room. What should she do? Her eyes fell on the large rocking horse.

It was old but beautiful. It had a leather saddle and bridle and a dapple-gray coat. Its dark eyes were large, and its mane and tail—made from real horsehair—were long and thick. Its legs were positioned as if it was moving. Wondering who it had belonged to, Mary scrambled onto its back. Holding the reins, she started to make it rock backward and forward, slowly at first, but getting higher every time, and as she did so, she shut her eyes and her imagination, which had been lying dormant, like a bulb in the winter soil, suddenly put out a green shoot. For a few precious, fleeting minutes, she forgot everything she hated about her new life and let her imagination transport her away. She wasn't Mary Lennox—the orphan from India who no one wanted or liked—she was beautiful Sita, escaping from an evil demon, carried by a winged horse across the bright blue Indian sky. . . .

5

Exploring Misselthwaite

W hen Mary finished playing with the horse,
she investigated the wooden chest in one
corner of the room. There were some very old
toys inside. Most of them didn't interest her—a
tin of metal soldiers with the paint peeling off, a
spinning top and a jack-in-the-box. But she did
take out a skipping rope with wooden handles.
She tried skipping a few steps in the room, but

realized she needed more space.

I could take it outside and skip in the gardens, she thought.

She peered around her bedroom door. Mrs. Medlock had told her that she could not explore, but why? *I'm not a prisoner,* she thought mutinously. *And this is my uncle's house. I'm sure he doesn't intend for me to be kept in my room at all times.*

She put the skipping rope in the large front pocket of her dress and set off down the corridor. She wasn't sure where she was going, but she felt it was important to show Mrs. Medlock that she was not going to be ordered around.

A pale light came in through the stone windows, illuminating the bare boards on the floor and the paintings on the walls. Mary looked out of the windows to the back of the house, expecting to see landscaped gardens, but to her surprise she saw a sea of mud and ruts. It looked as if some of the soldiers who had used the house during the war had been camped out there.

Mary remembered what Mrs. Medlock had said—*It's not the house it was. . . .*—and suddenly she felt sorry for the old place. It looked like it had once been loved, but now it was falling apart and neglected.

She continued on and reached a large open door. She peered inside and saw a room with a high ceiling, a polished wooden floor, and lots of bookshelves. It looked like it might once have been the library, but now it was stacked with chairs and tables and cases of stuffed animals. Mary shrank back into the shadows of the corridor as she saw her uncle and Mrs. Medlock standing by a pile of paintings at the far end of the room. They were in the middle of a heated discussion.

"It doesn't matter, Mrs. Medlock," Mary's uncle was saying. "These are of no importance."

"We can't just leave them all piled up like this,"

the housekeeper protested.

"Well, get rid of them, then. Throw them away. Burn them. I don't care!"

"But, sir." Mrs. Medlock picked up a portrait of a woman's head. "What about this one?"

Mary saw a muscle jump in her uncle's jaw. "Please," he said in a low voice. "I don't need to be reminded of her. She's gone."

Worried that he was about to leave the room and see her, Mary hurried on. She was desperate to feel fresh air on her face, to get out of the bleak, gloomy house where people were cranky and rude and peculiar. There was an avenue of trees to one side that led out onto the mist-covered moors, and she headed for it. The grass was overgrown, but the ground was flat. Mary pulled out her jump rope and began to skip along the path, counting her steps out loud.

She had just reached seventy-five and had emerged from the trees onto the moors, when she stopped. Through the swirling mist she could see a boy. He looked about a year older than her. He had dark curly hair and was carrying a lamb around his neck. She remembered what Martha had said. Maybe this boy was Martha's brother—Dickon.

Mary started toward the boy. "Hello? Are you Martha's brother?" But as she spoke, he turned and disappeared into the mist.

"Come back!" Mary commanded.

She started to run after him, but he'd vanished as if he'd never been there, and the mist was looking thicker than ever. "Stay inside when the mist is rolling on the moors," Mary whispered to herself, remembering Mrs. Medlock's words. With one last look, she turned and headed back toward the house.

By the time Mary reached the house, her stomach was grumbling. She had only eaten a little of the porridge that morning, and she felt very hungry.

She went inside and managed to find the kitchen. The cook, Mrs. Pitcher, was busy chopping vegetables.

"It's time for my luncheon, I believe," Mary announced. "Now I would like—"

The cook interrupted her with a good-natured smile. "Doesn't matter what you'd like, lass. You'll get what you're given in this house."

Mary looked at her in frustration. "You know, I really don't understand you people at all!"

The cook laughed but it wasn't a mean laugh, and Mary watched as she set to work making sandwiches with thickly cut white bread, a scraping of butter, and some sort of pink meat. She wrapped them in parchment paper and handed them and an apple to Mary. "There you go. Now out of my kitchen. I have too many things to do to have a young 'un like you cluttering up the place." She winked. "Some of us have work to do."

Mary took the food outside and found a spot among the trees that was less muddy. She sat down on a fallen tree trunk and unwrapped the parchment paper. She lifted a slice of bread off the top sandwich. What was the strange, smooth pink meat inside? She'd never seen anything like it. She pulled one of the slices off the bread and sniffed it warily. Putting out her tongue, she licked it and reacted with disgust. It tasted terrible! Was it even real meat?

She threw it away, but it landed quite close to her feet. Peeling the other slice off, she flung it farther. It sailed through the air and ended up near one of the other trees. Mary nibbled at a slice of bread. That at least was fresh—and tasty. She took a bigger bite.

A rustle made Mary look around. The branches of a bush were moving as if something was pushing its way through. Mary shrank back as a dog appeared, nose first, then muzzle, then a shaggy brown body.

"No! Go on! Go away!" Mary exclaimed, waving at it with a shooing motion. Most of the dogs in India were strays, and they were often dangerous.

The dog ignored her and trotted over to the piece of meat that had landed near the bushes. It sniffed it. "*No!* That's not for you!" Mary cried. The dog gobbled the meat up hungrily. "Now you're fed, you can go," said Mary, pulling her feet underneath her in case she had to jump up quickly. "Go on."

But the dog had spotted the second slice of meat that lay closer to her. "Oh, no," Mary said anxiously. "Don't you dare! It's far too near. I want you to go!"

She squealed as the dog leaped at the meat. Grabbing it in its jaws, it turned and raced away.

Mary watched it go. It had seemed almost as afraid of her as she had been of it. And it had looked as hungry as she was feeling too.

Finishing her bread and apple, she went around the back of the house and spent the afternoon exploring the grounds. Away from where the soldiers had camped, there were trees and ferns, overgrown shrubberies and winding gravel paths. Her boots were soon caked with mud, and her clothes were damp. Every so often, she heard a faint rustle behind her. The feeling she was being followed prickled her, and eventually, glancing over her shoulder, she saw the dog again. "Of all the silly things," she said, her face breaking into a smile as it looked at her with its pink tongue hanging out. "Are you following me?"

It wagged its tail.

"Mary!" Mrs. Medlock was ringing a bell and calling sharply through an open window in the house. Her voice carried across the grounds. "Mary! Where are you, child? Come here this instant!"

The dog vanished at the sound of Mrs. Medlock's voice.

With a sigh, Mary went back to the house. Mrs. Medlock was looking cranky. "I've been hunting high and low for you," she huffed. "In future, kindly remember your bath will be ready at five twenty-five p.m. and you will be expected to be in your room by then. Now upstairs with you." She marched on ahead of Mary.

"Do you have a problem with wild dogs around here?" Mary asked curiously, running after her.

"Wild dogs!" snorted Mrs. Medlock. "Of course we don't have a problem with wild dogs."

As Mary walked into her room, the door was shut firmly behind her. After being outside in the fresh air, and having space and freedom to skip and explore, her room felt more like a prison than ever. Going over to the walls, she touched the birds on the faded wallpaper. She imagined them fluttering their wings and flying away, sweeping her off to a place far away.

A forgotten memory suddenly surfaced in her mind. A flock of birds swooping around the garden in India. She had been very little—about four years old—and she'd run up to them. They'd flown away of course, but for a moment they had been all around her in flashes of brilliant color. She'd laughed in delight, spinning around with her arms above her head, until she heard a bang. It had been her mother, her face tearstained, abruptly closing the shutters of her window, shutting out Mary and the sound of her laughter. Mary could remember the confusion she'd felt. Didn't her mother like her to be happy?

Mary returned to the present. Her life in India was already starting to feel like a very long time ago, but her memories of the way her mother had looked that day—and every other day that Mary could remember—no, she didn't think those memories would ever fade.

6

Making Friends

That night, Mary was woken up by the same high-pitched wailing again. She listened, open-eyed in the dark. Was it the wind like Martha had said? Or was it a ghost of one of the soldiers who had died here? Remembering the fear she had felt the night before, she pulled the coverlet over her ears and stayed in bed.

When Mary woke in the morning, she sat up to

see Martha kneeling beside her fireplace, arranging a layer of paper on the ashes. A tray with more porridge was on her table.

"Hello, Martha," she said.

"Miss," Martha said coldly.

Mary remembered the noises in the night. "Were you here when the soldiers were, Martha? Did you work in the hospital?"

Martha didn't reply; she just kept laying the fire.

Mary realized that Martha was still upset with her. She wondered how she could get back the friendly Martha from the day before. Climbing out of bed, she knelt beside her. "Is there an order to how you put the fire together?" she asked.

"Yes, miss," said Martha, not looking at her as she started to put coal on the layer of paper.

Mary picked up a piece of coal. Its black coating stained her fingers, and the dust dropped onto the rug.

"Oh, miss, please don't!" exclaimed Martha, sounding exasperated. "You'll spoil the rug and your dress, and it'll be me who has to clean both."

Mary sighed. Helping Martha didn't seem to be making the maid any friendlier. She gave up, sat back on her heels, and changed the subject. "Martha. The noises I hear in the night—do dead soldiers haunt this house?"

For a second, Mary was sure she saw a look of alarm in the maid's eyes. "I'm sure I don't know what you're talking about. If you hear noises, then just turn over and go back to sleep. That's the best thing to do."

Mary was certain Martha knew more than she was admitting. She watched as Martha lit the fire in silence and then went to the door without saying another word.

Anger and unhappiness rushed through Mary at the thought of being left on her own again.

"I didn't ask to be here, you know!" she burst out angrily.

Martha looked back. "And Mr. Craven didn't ask to take you in, but he did all the same," she said calmly but firmly, and then she was gone, shutting the door behind her.

Mary stamped her foot. It seemed like the one person who might have talked to her in this dismal place now didn't want to. She glared at the closed door, feeling lonelier than she had ever felt in her life.

Later that morning, Mary put on her outdoor boots, a new warm blue coat, and matching hat and paid another visit to the kitchen.

"Mrs. Pitcher," she said to the cook, "you gave me sandwiches yesterday for my luncheon. I need the same meat in my sandwiches today." She hesitated. "Please?" she added, remembering her manners.

Mrs. Pitcher gave her a surprised look and then

nodded and took a loaf of bread from the counter.

"What is the meat you put inside the sand-wiches?" Mary asked curiously, watching her.

"Spam," said Mrs. Pitcher.

"Spam?" echoed Mary, trying out the un-familiar word.

The cook chuckled. "Yes, Spam." She quickly made the sandwiches. "Now go on, away with you," she said, shooing her out of the kitchen.

Mary pushed the sandwiches into her leather bag and hurried outside. She had a plan! No one in the house seemed to want to be her friend, but she had a feeling that maybe there was someone— or something—in the garden who would. What she would really have liked to be doing was exploring the upper floor of the house and solving the mys-tery of the night cries. The strange look Martha had given her that morning when she had men-tioned noises in the night had convinced her that something was being kept from her, and Mary was determined to find out what it was. But she didn't dare risk exploring and Mrs. Medlock finding her. She wasn't sure what the housekeeper would do if she found Mary "*poking about*," but she didn't want to find out.

I'll wait until tonight, she thought. *When everyone's asleep.*

In the meantime, she was going to concentrate on something else. She hurried to where she had eaten her lunch the day before. Feeling very daring, she unwrapped a sandwich and took out the Spam. She placed it in the exact same spot where she had thrown it before. Looking around hopefully, she retreated to the tree stump and sat down to wait. Where was the dog? She'd been sure it would be here, and even a dog as a friend would be better than nothing.

She waited and waited.

"Come on," she whispered. "Please come."

She heard a bark and saw that the shaggy brown

dog was standing in the bushes. "There you are!" she said, smiling as it trotted out and gobbled the meat up, watching her all the time.

"Hello," Mary said. She felt strange—she'd never talked to a dog before. But she decided that its eyes looked cleverer than those of many humans she had met. "What's your name, then?"

The dog gave a short woof.

Mary felt a flicker of anxiety. "Are you diseased?" There were some dogs in India that had a nasty sickness called rabies. They barked and foamed at the mouth and bit people. But this dog didn't look like it was dangerous. "Well?"

The dog barked again.

"You see, I've no idea if that means yes or no," Mary told it. "Very well. I shall start with a simpler question—are you a girl dog or a boy dog?"

The dog whined hopefully and put its head to one side.

"Oh, no," said Mary, realizing what it wanted.

"I'm saving the other slice for later. We'll have a play first. Do you think you would like that?"

The dog's tail wagged a little. Mary smiled. "I think you are a girl dog," she declared. "And I shall call you . . . Jemima! Come on, Jemima. Let's play!" Mary started to run. The dog hesitated for a moment and then raced after her.

It was the first time Mary had run outside since she'd arrived at Misselthwaite. She charged across the muddy ground. The dog bounded behind her, veering to one side and then overtaking her, leading the way down twisting paths that curved through the trees. Mary raced after her, her breath coming in pants as she drew in deep lungfuls of fresh air. It was wonderful to have someone who wanted to be with her! Water and mud splashed up from the puddles, and for the first time in ages she felt properly alive. A laugh burst out of her. The dog barked, and she barked back. The dog danced around her, barking three times. Mary copied her, spinning around, her face lifted to the sky.

The dog bounded to the bottom of a very high wall that was almost completely hidden by a curtain of creepers and disappeared. Mary stopped in surprise and ran to where she had been. She spotted a small hole under the wall. The dog must have crawled through it. "Jemima?" she called.

Nothing happened. Mary felt a wave of disappointment at losing her friend. She was about to turn to go when suddenly the dog's head reappeared. The dog barked as if she was encouraging Mary to follow.

"I can't follow you through there, Jemima," said Mary with a grin. "That hole's much too small for me. Is this where you live, then?"

The dog whined.

Mary glanced up. The high wall had a thick covering of ivy on top and a tree growing beside it.

What's on the other side? she wondered. *Maybe I could climb up and see. . . .*

Just then, there was the sound of the bell ringing in the distance and Mrs. Medlock's voice calling faintly, "Mary! Mary!"

Oh, bother, thought Mary crankily.

Mrs. Medlock's shouts and bell ringing grew more insistent.

Mary sighed and looked at the dog. "Tomorrow," she promised, putting the rest of the sandwich down on the ground for it to eat. "I'll see you then, Jemima. Make sure you come."

The dog barked, and Mary smiled as she turned away. Her heart felt much lighter as she skipped back to the house. She'd made a friend at Misselthwaite at last.

7

Colin

Mary ran up the grand staircase, moving as quietly as she could, her cotton dressing gown flapping. The wind was blowing hard outside the house that night, and the moon was the only source of light. Mary's heart was beating fast, but she had to solve the mystery of the wailing cry.

Reaching the second floor, she turned down a dark corridor with covered paintings and closed doors. As she padded along it, a gust of wind blew from a cracked window at the far end, and a dust sheet on a painting she was passing billowed up. Mary caught sight of the picture beneath and stopped in her tracks. It was a portrait of her mother! She held the dust sheet back and gazed at it, loss and guilt stabbing through her. Her mother looked about eighteen. She was sitting at a piano, smiling and happy, her dark hair falling in waves to her shoulders. Mary blinked. It felt wrong to see her mother like that. In all her memories, her mother was frowning and turning away.

She lifted the dust sheet on the next painting. It was another picture of her mother. This time she looked a few years older. She was sitting on a swing in a clearing, wearing a white dress, and there was another woman, the same age as her, in a blue dress. Something tugged at Mary's mind. She almost felt as if she'd been to that clearing, but it looked like it was in England, so that was impossible.

Intrigued, she looked closely at the other woman. She was very similar to Mary's mother, but slightly taller and her hair wasn't brown but a dark chestnut-red like Mary's. Mary knew it had to be her mother's twin sister, Grace, her uncle's dead wife. They hadn't been identical twins, but they looked very much alike.

Leaving the paintings, Mary tiptoed on and turned into a carpeted corridor with a grand mural on the wall. There was a bedroom door opposite her, and it was open. Whose bedroom was it? Curiously, she crept closer. Her eyes widened as she saw a dark-haired boy, about her age, asleep in an ornate bed.

He opened his eyes and looked at her. She leaped back out of sight.

"I saw you!" the boy's voice rang out.

Mary's thoughts raced. Who was he? He couldn't be a servant—the bedroom was far too grand. It was bigger and far more beautifully decorated than her own.

He spoke again. "I can't say I saw you enough to positively identify you, but I'm sure if I told them that I'd seen a little servant girl, they'd know who I meant and you'd be in firm trouble, wouldn't you?"

Servant girl? Well, whoever he was, Mary wasn't going to be called a servant. She marched into the bedroom, intending to give him a piece of her mind. There was a solid carved wooden bed with curtains draped at the back of it, two bedside tables, a reading stand, and a table and chairs. The boy lying in bed was wearing a vest and was propped up against some pillows. He looked just a little older than her. His brown hair fell across his forehead and his skin was very pale, as if he hadn't seen sunlight for a long time. Mary's attention was particularly caught by his dark eyes. They didn't look like a child's eyes—they were intense and wary.

"I'm no servant!" Mary exclaimed indignantly. "My name is Mary Lennox. My mother was twin sister to the mistress of this house and my uncle by marriage owns it still and you'll do well to give me the respect I'm due!"

"I'll give you none!" the boy declared just as haughtily. "I am Colin Craven. The uncle you speak of is *my* father, and if I were to live, this place would one day belong to me."

Mary felt a rush of shock. Whatever she had been expecting, it wasn't this.

"We're . . . *cousins*?" she said, not quite able to believe it.

The boy's eyes flicked back to hers. He studied her for a moment, and then a half smile pulled at his lips and he gave a brief nod.

"But I've never heard of you!" Mary said in astonishment.

"Nor I you," said the boy.

Mary had a feeling her cousin was as surprised as she was, but he was trying to be grown up and hide it.

"You're very thin," he said judgmentally.

"You're very white," responded Mary.

"You smile with no teeth," Colin challenged her.

"You don't smile at all!" retorted Mary.

"Why are you here?" demanded Colin.

"Why shouldn't I be?" said Mary defiantly.

Colin gave her a warning look. "I don't want a friend."

"Good. I've plenty already," said Mary, shrugging.

She took a breath, and then a laugh burst out of her. She couldn't help it. This new cousin might be rather strange and very prickly, but it felt miraculous to be talking properly to someone her own age! Colin's lips twitched into a brief smile too, and she had a feeling he was enjoying their conversation as much as she was.

"So you're the one who cries out at night," said Mary, drawing closer. "I thought it was a ghost, that this house was cursed—"

"You think this house is cursed?" interrupted Colin.

Mary nodded. "Yes, by all the soldiers who died here."

"No," said Colin, shaking his head. "It is cursed but not by the soldiers. The curse came before the war. The reason people say this house is cursed is because it killed my mother and now it intends to kill me as well."

"My mother's dead too." The guilty secret Mary had been carrying around inside her, the secret she couldn't even let herself think about, suddenly burst out of her. "I killed her!"

Mary knew this was true. She had wished her mother dead, and her wish had come true. She stared at Colin, wondering how he would react.

He looked at her doubtfully. "Did you really?"

Mary nodded.

Colin sighed and then spoke in a strangely grown-up voice. "Well then, we both know trag-edy, don't we?"

Feeling relieved that he hadn't judged her or said she was awful, Mary edged a step closer.

"What did you mean—this house intends to kill you?" she asked.

Colin's face closed like a clam. "I do not wish to speak about it," he said curtly, turning his head away from her. "You may go now."

Mary was taken aback at the sudden change in him, but if this strange new cousin thought she was going to beg and plead to be allowed to stay with him, he could think again. She lifted her chin. "Very well." She walked to the door and looked back over her shoulder. "I suppose you may see me again," she said airily. "Or you may not."

"But . . ." Colin began.

"Good night," said Mary, and she left the room.

"Come back!" she heard Colin exclaim indignantly.

Mary smiled to herself. So it was just as she'd thought: he hadn't really wanted her to leave. Well, good. He needed to learn he couldn't order her around. Not if they were going to be friends. *Friends!* With an excited spring in her step at the thought, she hurried back to her own bedroom.

That night, Mary dreamed of India again. This time she was giggling as her father chased her, pretending to be a tiger. "I'm going to get you!" he growled. "Where are you, little monkey?"

Mary dived into her mother's bedroom. Her mother wasn't there. Where to hide? She pulled the wardrobe open, but it was too full of beautiful dresses. She looked under the bed, but there wasn't enough space and so she jumped under the covers and lay as still as she could.

She heard someone enter the room. She tensed in delight. Daddy was going to find her! Footsteps came over to the bed, and the covers were raised. Mary opened her mouth to squeal, but it wasn't her father who was staring at her—it was her mother and her eyes were harsh and cold. Mary scrambled out of the bed and fled. . . .

Mary was woken up by Martha shaking her by the shoulder. "Wake up, girl!"

Mary sat up, her hair tousled. As she opened her eyes, she remembered the events of the night before, but before she could ask Martha about the cousin everyone had been keeping secret from her, the maid handed her a new dress—a navy one with smocking on the front. It was the smartest in Mary's wardrobe.

"There's no time to waste. The master wants to see you."

Mary stretched and got up slowly. Martha helped her into her clothes. "Now eat your porridge before Mrs. Medlock comes."

Mary played with her spoon in the porridge as Martha tidied away her nightclothes.

"Come on, girl. You can eat faster than that," Martha urged, picking up a hairbrush. "My mother would say you're doing as little as fast as you can."

Mary began to eat more quickly as Martha pulled the brush through her hair, parting it at the side. "I've decided I like your mother," Mary said.

Martha gave her an exasperated look. "You've

never met her. Now eat."

Mary ate another few spoonfuls. "I have decided I like your brother, Dickon, too." She thought about the boy she had seen in the mist. "And I *have* met him. Or at least I would have done, but he ran off. I'd like to meet him properly." She sighed glumly. "Though I imagine he wouldn't like me. No one does. Well, almost no one," she added, thinking about Colin. She decided she would keep him secret for a while, at least until she found out why no one at Misselthwaite had told her about him.

"You say no one likes you, but how do you like yourself, girl?" Martha asked.

Mary frowned. "What do you mean?"

Martha put the brush down. "Mother said it to me once when I was in a bad temper. She turned on me and said, 'There you stand, saying you don't like this and you don't like that, but how do you like yourself right now, lass?'"

The door suddenly opened, and Mrs. Medlock marched in. Mary saw Martha's eyes widen in alarm.

"Not that I want to interrupt this little reminiscence," the housekeeper said, fixing Martha with a withering look, "but there are those who are waiting on us."

"Mrs. Medlock, I . . . I'm sorry," Martha stammered. "I—"

"It's not Martha's fault," Mary interrupted, not wanting Martha to get into trouble. "I was being tardy. She was scolding me for it."

Martha shot Mary a surprised but grateful look.

Mrs. Medlock sniffed sourly. "It doesn't matter whose fault it is. What matters is that you're late. Now come along, child." She strode out of the room. "The master is waiting."

8

Mr. Craven

"Now, when the master speaks to you, you are to answer back with a 'sir,' you understand?" Mrs. Medlock instructed.

"Yes, Mrs. Medlock," said Mary, trying to keep up with her as she marched down the corridor.

The housekeeper stopped outside a heavy wooden door. "And say nothing fanciful. He has enough concerns. And do *not* stare." She knocked and a bell rang from the inside. Mrs. Medlock gave Mary a warning nod and then opened the study door.

Mary walked in bravely. The gloomy room was large and dark, heavy curtains partly pulled across the windows, shutting out the daylight. There was a huge desk at one end with a reading light on it, and the wall behind was completely covered with pictures and display cases containing stuffed animals and birds. Mary's uncle was sitting at the desk.

"Come here, girl," he commanded. "Into the light where I can see you."

She stepped forward, her attention caught by his hunchback. She looked away quickly, her eyes falling on a photo on his desk in a silver frame. It was a picture of Aunt Grace and Colin when he was a little boy. Her uncle saw her looking at it and quickly turned it facedown.

He spoke gruffly. "Mrs. Medlock tells me you're cluttering up the place. She would have me send you to school."

Mary had never been to school, but she hated the thought of being surrounded by other children day and night. She spoke firmly. "I would not like that, sir. I like it here."

Her uncle studied her. "Then we will find you a governess."

"No, I have no need for a governess," Mary said quickly. "I have too much to learn at Misselthwaite." She paused and then added, "Sir."

Her uncle frowned. "This house has nothing to teach a child."

Mary knew she had to convince him not to send her away to school or to get a governess. "But I want to play out of doors and explore the grounds. It was too hot to do that in India."

He tapped a pen on the desk. "Mary, I'm obliged

by law to have you taught."

Mary met his eyes. "Then we need to break the law, wouldn't you say?"

Her uncle's eyebrows rose slightly as their gazes locked. "Mrs. Medlock says she can see Alice—your mother—in you."

"Did she like my mother?" Mary asked curiously. "For she doesn't seem to like me."

Her uncle didn't answer her question. "It is not your *mother* I see," he said finally, looking away quietly.

Mary frowned but then understood. "Do you mean I remind you of my aunt—your wife? My mother once told me that I was like my aunt, Grace, too."

It was an extremely hazy memory. She had been very young and chasing a large butterfly, giggling and laughing. She could remember her mother scooping her up in her arms. "You are so like

Grace, little Mary," she had said, laughing. "I cannot wait for her to meet you!" It was the only time Mary could remember her mother hugging her.

Her uncle studied her and then nodded. "Very well. I've reached a decision. You do not have to go to school. But if you cause me any trouble, I will send you away in an instant, do you understand?"

Mary nodded calmly although inside she felt like she was jumping with excitement at having gotten her own way. "Yes, sir," she said politely.

"You won't be here long anyway," her uncle sighed. "All women are destined to leave Misselthwaite, one way or another." He turned away and waved a hand at her. "Go on. Off you go."

When Mary left the study, Mrs. Medlock was waiting outside. Mary walked straight past her. "I am not to be sent to school," she said over her shoulder. "And I'm not to have a governess." She bit back her grin.

Mrs. Medlock hurried after her. "Are you not?" she said in surprise.

"No," Mary said. "Mr. Craven's orders. He doesn't want me to leave this house like all the other womenfolk."

"What?" Mrs. Medlock threw an astonished glance back at the study door.

"Please be sure to have Mrs. Pitcher supply me with my special sandwiches," Mary said firmly. "I need extra meat because I need to grow."

Mrs. Medlock gaped, and unable to hide her smile, Mary dashed away to her room.

Later that morning, Mary returned to the fallen tree trunk where she had first met Jemima the dog. It was a bright day and the sky had hints of blue, although thick white clouds still scudded across it. Mary peeled apart the sandwiches that Cook had given her and took out one of the pieces of Spam.

"I know you're there!" she called, looking at the bushes, but the branches didn't move.

"If you think I'm throwing any of the pieces today, you're wrong. You'll come out and eat like a polite animal—from my hand," Mary said.

The dog poked her brown head out from behind a tree stump.

Mary smiled and held out the meat. The dog came over, slowly at first, but breaking into a trot as she got closer. Wagging her shaggy tail, she ate the Spam from Mary's hand, licking her fingers as she did so. Mary giggled as she felt Jemima's rough tongue. She fed her more of the slices, and then Jemima let her stroke her ears and face.

"You are a very nice dog, Jemima. Where have you come from?"

Jemima backed away. Cocking her head to one side, she looked at Mary and barked.

"Do you want to play again? Come on, then!"

said Mary eagerly. Shoving the remains of the sandwich in her leather bag, she raced away with the dog at her heels. They charged through the gardens and down the grassy paths toward the moors.

As they reached the end of the avenue, Jemima raced into the mist. "Wait, Jemima! We shouldn't go on the moors!" Mary cried.

CRACK!

There was a shrill howl, and Mary's heart skipped a beat. She ran toward the noise and saw Jemima had her leg caught in a horrible metal trap—the type poachers used to catch rabbits and hares.

"No!" gasped Mary.

Jemima's yelps of pain stabbed through Mary like a knife. The metal jaws of the trap were crushing the poor dog's leg, and her eyes looked wild. As Mary crouched down, Jemima snapped at her, mad with pain. Mary jumped back in alarm.

Jemima struggled, hurting her leg even more as she did so.

"No, don't, please don't!" Mary begged, tears welling in her eyes.

She knelt down again but more slowly this time. She murmured soothingly, trying to keep her voice from shaking. "It's all right, Jemima. I'm going to help you. I promise. Please let me."

The dog stopped struggling, standing still now, but shivering in pain. Her dark eyes looked pleadingly up at Mary.

"That's it," Mary said cautiously. "Stay still."

Her eyes darted over Jemima's horribly wounded leg. The blood made her feel queasy, but she had to help. Swallowing hard, she leaned forward and took hold of the jaws of the trap. Using all her strength, she forced them apart, loosening their grip on Jemima's leg. With a yelp, the dog pulled her leg free.

As she did so, the jaws of the trap sprang back together. Mary let go just in time. She gulped—her hand had almost gotten trapped—but she'd done it. She had freed Jemima!

Jemima was licking at her wound. She stood up, but she couldn't put any weight on her damaged leg.

"Come here. Let me help you," Mary said, but Jemima hobbled away from her. Mary ran after her, but although the dog could only use three legs, she could still move faster than Mary and seemed determined not to be caught. She raced through the grounds to the hole under the wall and disappeared.

I can't leave her, Mary thought. *She's injured. She needs help.*

She looked up at the ivy and at the tree growing next to the high wall, then she made a decision. Ignoring the twigs that scratched at her legs through her stockings and tore at her hands, she scrambled up into the tree and started to climb. Up and up she went, finding footholds for her feet and heaving herself until she reached the very top of the wall. With a final wriggle, she pulled herself onto it and straddled it as if she was riding a horse.

Triumph rushed through her. She was so high up! Now all she had to do was climb down the other side of the wall. There were tree branches and creepers on that side too. Mary swung her leg over and started to clamber down, again finding footholds for her feet. But as she let go of the top of the wall, the branch she had just put her weight on snapped.

With a shriek, Mary felt herself start to fall!

9

The Secret Garden

The creepers grabbed at Mary, slowing her descent as she crashed down through a tunnel of foliage. She landed with a bump at the top of a steep slope and then tumbled all the way down it, rolling over and over through the dead leaves and bracken. She thumped to a stop and lay there for a moment, wondering if she had broken anything. Feeling dazed, she blinked her eyes. A faint, ghostly, dark-haired woman in a long dress was leaning over her, looking worried.

"Mother!" gasped Mary in shock. She sat bolt upright, and the figure dissolved into sunlight.

Mary drew in a trembling breath. She must have bumped her head in the fall. For a moment, she had really thought her mother was there, but of course she couldn't be.

Where am I? she wondered, looking around. Trees surrounded her, their branches meeting overhead. Through a gap in the leafy canopy, the sun shone down between the leaves, casting dappled light on the ground around her.

Mary got slowly to her feet. She had cuts and grazes, and her new coat was covered with moss and leaves, but nothing hurt too badly. She set off down a path. "Jemima!" she called, wondering where her friend was.

The trees were ancient—almost prehistoric—and

their trunks seemed to have exploded in all directions. Their twisted branches were covered with a layer of soft green moss that seemed to glow in the sunlight. Leaves lay in a thick, dry carpet, and Mary's feet crunched through them as she clambered over fallen tree trunks and skirted around the knobbly roots that had grown up through the ground. Her skin tingled. *It's like a place from a fairy tale,* she thought.

She passed tall, craggy rocks dripping with water and reached a jungle of enormous green plants that towered over her head. They had stems as thick as tree trunks and leaves as big as umbrellas. They blocked her way, but she pushed through them until she emerged into a sunny clearing. The long meadow grass was as high as her waist in places, and there was a wide stream on the far side with rocky banks, its water reflecting the sunlight. Mary waded through the grass toward it. As she reached it, she heard a woof and felt a rush of delight. Jemima was on the other side of the stream, her injured leg held up protectively underneath her.

"Jemima!" Mary called.

The dog gave Mary a suspicious look and backed away.

"No, you can't be cranky with me," Mary pleaded. "That trap wasn't my fault. Come on, come back and we'll get that wound better for you."

Jemima held her gaze but didn't move, so Mary came to a decision.

"Very well." If Jemima wouldn't come to her, then she would go to Jemima! She pulled off her coat and bag, and leaving them on the grass, she stepped into the clear water, gasping at the coldness. The water got deeper and deeper until she realized she was going to have to swim. She wasn't very good at swimming, but she struck out and swam determinedly to the far side. Reaching the bank, she pulled herself out of the water, shivering with the cold.

Jemima watched her warily.

"Can I see your paw now, Jemima?" Mary said.

The dog didn't move.

"I promise I won't hurt you," Mary said. She took a step toward her, and Jemima took a step away. Mary sighed. "You don't want help? Very well, then. We'll deal with your paw later. First, we'll explore. This is such a mysterious place! Come on."

She walked past Jemima, and Jemima followed her on three legs. Mary broke into a run and Jemima overtook her, leading the way. She still seemed to be able to move just as fast on three legs as four.

There was so much to see in this garden that was hidden away behind the wall. They raced past giant tree ferns, through a grove of strange trees with bulbous trunks and frond-like leaves, and wriggled their way through junglelike foliage.

As Mary pushed the leaves aside, a story bubbled up inside her. "There were once two friends called Mary and Jemima!" she cried. "And they discovered a strange but beautiful garden together. They stayed there and played in it all day long!"

They emerged into a formal area with overgrown flower beds, gravel paths, and stone statues covered with ivy. At the far end was a beautiful sunken temple—an old building of gray stone arches with no roof. Mary and Jemima ran over to it.

"Oh, Jemima! Look!" said Mary, gazing in delight at the ankle-deep pool in the center of the temple, which shimmered and gleamed, reflecting the light. The dog barked excitedly, and Mary barked back, happiness filling her.

Jemima leaped into the pool. Mary followed, and they splashed joyfully through the water, spraying droplets in all directions. Jumping out, they hurried on together until they reached a grassy clearing with overgrown mounds of scarlet flowers and red-barked dogwood trees all around. Mary sank back in the grass, panting for breath. Why was this garden hidden away behind such a high wall? Gardens weren't usually secret places. They were for people to walk in and enjoy, but this place felt as if no one had been in it for a very long time.

Hearing a bird singing, Mary glanced around. A robin with a bright red breast was perched on top of an old stone statue of a giant broken head that was covered with thick moss. The robin gave her a beady look and twittered again.

"Hello to you too," said Mary with a smile, wondering if it was the same robin she had seen when she'd first arrived at Misselthwaite.

The robin sang and fluttered its wings. Mary

had the strangest feeling that it was trying to tell her something "What is it?" she asked.

The little bird flew into the statue's open mouth. Then it popped its head out and twittered at Mary again. Jemima barked.

Mary was sure that both animals were trying to get her to do something. She scrambled to her feet and went over to the statue. The robin's insistent singing grew louder as Mary got closer, and she had the strangest feeling that it was encouraging her.

"Is there something inside there?" she whispered. "Something you want me to find." Standing on tiptoes, she reached into the mouth. She felt dry moss, and then her fingertips touched something hard and metallic. What was it? It was just too far for her to reach.

Jemima woofed beside her. Mary looked down and saw that the dog had fetched a stick. She dropped it at Mary's feet.

Mary smiled. It was just what she needed! "That's as good an idea as any you've had, Jemima!"

Picking the stick up, Mary stuck it in the hole and used it to fish the metal object out. As she pulled it into the daylight, she saw that it was a large iron key covered with moss. She brushed the moss away and looked at it in astonishment. What was a key doing hidden in the statue's mouth, and what did it unlock?

"Well?" she asked the animals. "Is that what you wanted me to find? What do I do with it?" Jemima jumped around on three legs, barking, and the robin sang.

"I don't know what you both mean," said Mary with an exasperated laugh. She looked around at the sunlight falling on the garden, the giant green ferns and protective ancient trees. "But this place—this garden—it's amazing." She longed to explore some more, but just then, she heard the faint sound of a bell ringing and Mrs. Medlock calling her name from far away.

"I'm going to have to go," she said in frustration, putting the key in her pocket. "But I'll come back tomorrow. I promise. I need to have a look at your leg, Jemima. I hope it's going to heal." A thought struck her. "Now how do I get out of here?"

Jemima woofed and trotted away into a nearby copse of trees. Mary followed her and found that she was back where she had started. Picking up her coat and bag, she put them on, then scrambled up the bank to the base of the wall. She began to climb. At one point, her foot slipped, but she felt a branch suddenly meet it and boost her upward. Her eyes widened. It was almost as though the tree was helping her! It seemed impossible, but Mary was beginning to think anything could happen in this enchanting abandoned garden!

At the top of the wall, she paused for a moment and looked back. The garden stretched out like a secret kingdom. What a wonderful, amazing place. . . .

"Mary!" she heard Mrs. Medlock shout.

With a sigh, Mary swung her leg over the wall and scrambled down. On this side—the house side—everything seemed so much duller, so much grayer. Here a dog would be just a dog and a robin just a robin, but Mary didn't mind. She knew that the garden would be waiting for her—and her heart sang.

Mary was so excited about the garden that she didn't even care when Mrs. Medlock scolded her severely for returning late with her new coat all covered in mud.

"Look at you, girl! You've got dirt all over you. Your hair's matted—and wet!"

Mary shrugged. "Mr. Craven said to play. Well, I've been playing."

A little while later, as she lay in the steaming bath, soaking away the dirt, Mary looked at the key that she had smuggled into the bathroom. Why had Jemima and the robin wanted her to find it? Maybe there was a door into the garden and this key unlocked it. She felt like she was going to burst with her secret. If only there was someone she could tell. . . .

She thought of her cousin Colin lying in his bed upstairs. Her other secret. Maybe she would tell him about the garden. In fact, he might know about it already. After all, Colin had lived at Misselthwaite his entire life.

I'll go and see him tonight, thought Mary, and with a feeling of happy satisfaction, she slid under the steaming water.

10

Cousins

Mary was creeping cautiously along the corridor toward Colin's room that night when she heard someone coming. She hid in a doorway and listened. Colin's bedroom door opened.

"No, please, Mrs. Medlock!" she heard him beg. "I don't like it. It tastes horrible. It makes my stomach burn."

"I know you don't like it, Colin," said Mrs.

Medlock, "but your father says you must have it. It's going to make you well."

Mary heard Colin sob. "It won't. Nothing will. Please . . ."

"Colin, it's either the medicine or the brace," said Mrs. Medlock firmly. "Now come along. Be good and it will soon be over."

Colin screamed and Mary swallowed, feeling her own insides twist. Although she had heard the cries before, it was different now she knew that it was Colin making them. Her hands balled into fists. She wanted to run in and shout at Mrs. Medlock, to grab the medicine from her and throw it away so Colin never had to take it again. Why did he need medicine anyway? He was pale and thin, but he didn't look dreadfully ill.

After a few minutes, Mary heard Mrs. Medlock leaving. "I shall come back later, when you've calmed down," she said, shutting the door with a shake of her head.

Mary pressed herself into the shadows. She could only imagine how much trouble she'd be in if she was found. She waited a few more minutes and then crept along the corridor and opened Colin's door.

He jumped. There were tears on his face. He wiped them with his hand and turned away from her. She could tell he was trying to compose himself, that he didn't want her to see him crying.

"Sometimes I need to be medicated." He spoke in a stiff, stilted voice as if he felt the need to explain. "My father says it's for my own benefit. I never see him. He's much too busy, but it's what the doctors told him." He took a breath and turned to look at her. "I thought you wouldn't visit again."

"I decided I wanted to," Mary said.

Her eyes fell on something on the far side of the room—a wheelchair! She hadn't noticed it the day before. She went over and sat down in it. "Is this your chair? Can't you walk? Is that why you have it?"

"That is not your business. Don't touch it!" Colin said crankily.

"It moves well," said Mary, swinging from side to side in it. "Do you want me to help you into it, then we can go and explore together? I could push you!"

"No!" Colin said. "I don't use it much because of my back. You've seen my father's hunchback; well, mine is the same, only much worse. I've never been able to walk." He sighed deeply. "Mary, I'm afraid to say your cousin is dying!"

The words sprang out of Mary's mouth before she could stop them. "You don't look like someone who's dying."

Colin sniffed peevishly. "How many dying people have you seen?"

Mary didn't answer. Her mind was too busy

turning over what he'd just said. If he really was dying, why didn't he look more ill? She'd only seen him sitting in bed, but he didn't appear to have a really bad hunchback. And why did he sound almost proud that he was dying? Something wasn't right.

"We could go outside?" she suggested. "That might make you feel better."

"Outside?" Colin echoed as if she'd suggested going to the moon. "I can't do that." He put a hand dramatically to his throat. "They tried to take me outside once, and the stench of the roses nearly killed me!"

Mary couldn't hold back her grin. "You're telling me you're afraid of flowers?" Her cousin glared at her. "That really isn't very sensible."

She could see he was cranky that she wasn't taking him seriously.

"What if I was to tell you that there's a paradise

out there?" she went on. "Where the birds sing for you and a friendly dog plays with you?"

"I'd say you were lying," Colin said. "And," he went on, his voice rising, "I'd say that I'm not interested, even if you are telling the truth. I am not interested in anything outside!"

"But . . ." Mary began.

Colin turned away. "I'm tired now. You may go."

Mary's mouth dropped open. How dare he order her around, particularly after she had just told him something so wonderful! "What?"

"I'm tired," Colin repeated. "Please leave."

"No." Mary folded her arms and felt a stab of satisfaction as Colin gave her a shocked look. He clearly wasn't used to having his commands ignored. "I am not your play toy, to be put down when you choose!" she told him.

"You came here to me. I didn't invite you," he said.

"I told you secrets," she retorted. "About my magic place."

"Secrets I didn't care to know of!" He sat bolt upright. "Now get out and leave me alone," he ordered, pointing to the door.

"Oh, you're insufferable!" Mary snapped, marching over to it.

"And you use words you don't understand!" Colin exclaimed.

Mary looked back, and their eyes met. In that moment, Mary felt a strong connection surge between them. *We're really quite alike,* she realized suddenly. *Not in all ways but in some. We . . . we belong together.*

Colin sank back against his pillows, and some of the tension seemed to leave the room.

Mary glanced at a portrait of Aunt Grace on the wall near the door. "Is that your mother?" she asked. "They say I look like her."

"I hate her," Colin muttered.

"Hate her?" Mary echoed, confused.

Colin nodded. "For dying. She loved me hugely, but then she died and left me all alone—is that not unforgivable of her?" He gave Mary a self-pitying look, clearly expecting sympathy.

But she had none to give. "At least your mother loved you," she said sharply. "My mother never loved me!" She stared at the floor.

There was a long silence.

When Colin spoke, his voice was softer. "Will you read to me while I try to fall asleep, Mary? I struggle to sleep. My back hurts, and I think too much." She glanced up and saw he was looking at her almost pleadingly.

She nodded and then returned to his bed and sat in the wheelchair beside it. "Very well. I will tell you a story of gods and a quarrel over who first made fire."

Colin snorted in disgust. "That sounds terrible."

He gave her a book. "Here, read me this instead."

A laugh burst out of Mary.

"What?" Colin said in surprise.

She shook her head. "I think you might quite possibly be the rudest boy I have ever met!"

Colin opened his mouth indignantly. Mary raised her eyebrows at him, and he subsided. Opening the book, she began to read.

11

Dreams and Memories

Mary read on until Colin's eyes closed, and then she got up and tiptoed out of his room.

As she pushed his door shut, she froze as she heard the sound of merry laughter behind her. Swinging around, she saw two ghostly figures running up the corridor—two young women in long white ball gowns—her mother and Aunt Grace. They smiled at her and vanished into thin air.

Mary blinked, icy fingers running up and down her spine. Had she really just seen two ghosts? *I must have imagined it,* she thought, staring at the empty corridor. *Mustn't I?*

Just then, a different noise made her jump—it was the sound of Mrs. Medlock coming upstairs again. *No!* She was going to be caught! Mary dashed to a nearby door on the opposite side of the corridor to Colin's and turned the handle. To her relief, it opened, and she slipped inside the large room.

Moonlight was shining in through the windows, bright enough for her to see that the walls were covered with detailed murals—painted scenes. The room was neat and tidy. Objects were set out around it as if they were on display—an ornate oriental screen, a wooden chest painted with flowers, display cabinets filled with carved ivory, and little elephants made from black wood.

Walking curiously around the room, Mary noticed a line of pale light on one of the walls. Going over, she realized that it was the outline of a hidden door. Excitement bubbled up inside her. Where did it lead? She carefully traced her fingers in the groove around the door until they snagged on a slightly raised piece of wood. She pressed it, and with a faint click, the door swung open.

Mary caught her breath as she gazed inside. The room on the other side seemed to shine and glow with light. The moonbeams streaming in through the large window were reflecting off swathes of thick white cobwebs hanging from the ceiling. There were dressmaker's dummies arranged around the room, clothed in beautiful, old-fashioned gowns, all decorated with gems that glittered brightly. Other dummies were piled with elegant cloaks and fur stoles. Mary stepped inside the room, her eyes widening in awe as she walked between the gowns, gently touching the soft, silky fabrics.

There was a pile of photographs and pictures stacked against each other in the center of the room along with boxes of photographs. Mary looked through them curiously. They were all of her mother and her aunt from when they were children through to when they were adults—her mother sitting with her twin sister's arms around her, the two sisters running through woodland and dancing in a field. In every picture, her mother and her aunt looked wonderfully happy. Mary paused at one of them walking away along a path lined with beautiful flower beds and statues. They were with two very young children and were all walking hand in hand, their backs to the camera. There was another picture of them all sitting under a big oak tree that had a swing attached to one of its branches.

Mary drifted away from the photographs and opened a wardrobe. It was filled with even more beautiful dresses. As she riffled through them, a few fell from the hangers and spilled onto the floor. Picking up a silver one, Mary couldn't resist trying it on. She slipped it over her nightclothes. It was much too big for her, but she spun around in it.

Once there was a girl called Mary Lennox, she thought dreamily. *She was invited to a grand ball, and when she was there, she danced and danced and everyone thought she was beautiful.* She whisked a feather boa from one of the dummies, sending the rest of the scarves and stoles tumbling to the floor, and then danced over to the chest of drawers and pulled open the heavy drawers one by one, finding folded lace, the softest leather gloves, tortoiseshell hair combs, and finally a drawer of jewelry boxes. Opening one, she took out a string of pearls and put them on.

She smiled at herself in the looking glass.

But then a familiar cry of pain made her remember exactly where she was. Colin! Mrs. Medlock must be in his room, forcing him to have more of the medicine he hated.

Mary shrugged off the dress and boa, and leaving them on the floor with the rest of the clothes, she hurried back into the first room and listened at the door. As she did so, she put her hand to her neck. She still had the pearls! She pulled them off and dropped them into the pocket of her dressing gown. She'd put them back later. Colin's screams had turned to sobs now, and she could hear Mrs. Medlock leaving. As her footsteps echoed away down the stairs, Mary pushed the door open, intending to go to Colin, but just then, a sound on the landing made her hesitate.

She peeped out. Her uncle was walking quickly toward Colin's room from the other end of the corridor. He arrived at Colin's door and stopped. His hand reached for the door, but then he pulled it back, his face a mass of conflicting emotions.

Why isn't he going in? thought Mary in astonishment. She knew that if she had been in pain and her father still alive, he would have rushed to her side.

Taking a deep breath, her uncle ran his hand through his hair, then turned and walked slowly back the way he had come.

At that moment, Mary hated her uncle with a passion. Why hadn't he gone in and comforted Colin? Colin's mother might have loved him, but his father obviously didn't.

With her uncle and Mrs. Medlock out and about in the corridors, Mary didn't dare risk going into Colin's room again. Instead, she hurried back to her own bedroom. So much had happened that day—Jemima being caught in the trap, finding the garden and the hidden room with all those clothes and photographs, Colin telling her he was going to die. Mary thought about the photograph of her mother and aunt holding hands with two young children. Could it possibly have been her and Colin in the photo? But no. Colin had said he'd never been able to walk, and the girl couldn't have been her because she'd never been to England. So who were those children?

When Mary fell asleep, images filled her head— flashes of the secret garden, the dog, the robin . . . She was running through the flower beds. The weeds had gone, and they were now filled with enormous bright flowers . . . and as she burst through them, she was suddenly in India again. Daddy was chasing her, pretending to be a monster, and she was giggling with delight. . . . Now she was sitting on the veranda. She had an exercise book on her knee, and it was filled with writing.

The door opened, and through it she could see her mother lying on a daybed. Their eyes met, and Mary felt a surge of hope. Maybe this time Mother would see her?

"I have written a story, Mother!" she called, going to the door. "Can I read it to you?"

"No, Mary. Not now. Please go away," her mother said wearily. "I need peace and quiet."

"But, Mother, I wrote it for you. . . ."

Her mother motioned to a servant in the room, and the door was shut in Mary's face.

She hates me, Mary thought, two tears escaping and spilling down her cheeks.

"Mary?" It was her father. He jumped up onto the veranda and saw her tears. "Oh, monkey," he said, wiping them away with his thumb. "Did you want to see Mother?" Mary nodded and he sighed. "She . . . she can't see you at the moment. She's sad."

"But I could try and make her happy, Daddy," said Mary.

He gave her a rueful smile. "I'm afraid that's not going to work, monkey. Seeing you makes her feel worse. Try not to take it to heart."

Mary didn't understand. Why would the sight of her make her mother feel worse?

"Your mother is sick," her father went on sadly. "So sick."

Mary scowled. "I wish she'd just get on and die and leave us all alone!"

"Mary, you mustn't speak like that!" her father said sharply. "Now be a good girl and run along. I need to go to work."

Mary had held in her tears. She would be a good girl like her father asked because, if she wasn't, well, maybe Daddy would start shutting doors on her and stop loving her too.

Mary woke to the sound of Martha cleaning out the grate in the fireplace. "Morning, miss," she said, giving Mary a friendly smile as Mary sat up in bed.

"Good morning, Martha," said Mary. She watched the maid work for a moment. "Martha? Have you worked here long?"

"Ever since I were twelve, miss. I started here as a scullery maid. Things were very different back in them days. There were scullery maids and parlor maids, footmen, a butler, stable boys." She shook her head. "They were different times, miss."

"Before the war," said Mary.

"And before the mistress died," said Martha quietly. "It's hard to believe now, but this house was once filled with light, laughter, happiness."

"What was my aunt, Grace, like?" Mary asked curiously.

Martha looked surprised. "Didn't your mother talk of her at all?"

"No. She never talked about England. Not that I can remember anyway," said Mary.

"Maybe it pained her too much," said Martha

with a sigh. "She and the mistress, thick as thieves they were. The crying that happened when it was announced that your father was going to be sent to India. . . ." She shook her head. "I'll never forget it. I don't know how your mother coped to lose the mistress when she died. It must have half killed her." She stood up. "Do you need anything else, miss?"

"No," said Mary, seeing that her porridge was on the table. She smiled. "I can manage now, Martha. Thank you."

Looking surprised but pleased, Martha left. Mary got herself clothed, choosing a dress that had no buttons at the back, then she sat down to eat her porridge. She thought about everything that Martha had said. She'd never realized her mother and Aunt Grace had been so close. It must have been terribly hard for her mother to leave England. Even more terrible must have been the news that

Aunt Grace had died.

The dream she'd had the night before came back into Mary's head. She knew it wasn't just a dream—it was a memory too. She could remember waiting on the veranda and the unhappiness that had surged through her when the door had been shut in her face. But for the first time, she wondered if maybe her mother had been unhappy too—grieving for her sister who had died. Thinking that made Mary feel a little differently about her mother.

Mary was still pondering it when she went outside. She'd managed to get some more Spam sandwiches from Cook, and she headed into the gardens. As she walked down a path, she heard a crack behind her. Her heart thumped. Was someone following her?

She slipped behind a huge oak tree and found a space underneath a cavernous rhododendron bush. Hiding under its branches, she watched as Mrs. Medlock came past, looking suspiciously left and right.

Oh, thought Mary with a slight smile, *so Mrs. Medlock is on my trail and thinks she is clever enough to spy on me, does she? Well, we shall see about that!*

12

Dickon

Mary waited until Mrs. Medlock came back along the path, looking cranky as she retraced her steps. Once she had vanished from sight, Mary emerged from the bush and continued on her way, calling for Jemima.

The dog didn't appear, but Mary caught sight of a figure in the mist. It was Martha's brother, Dickon. Anger surged through her. She was sure he was the one who was responsible for setting the trap—for injuring Jemima!

"Dickon? Stop!" she said, marching toward him.

Dickon started to step away.

"Oh, no you don't!" Mary cried. "Unless you want me to instruct your sister to box your ears. . . ."

Dickon stopped. "Martha wouldn't do that. She loves me plenty more than you."

"And would she still love you if she knew you'd been setting traps and poaching?" Mary demanded furiously.

Dickon marched toward her indignantly, and she saw there was a white stoat poking its head out of the top pocket of his green jacket. "Poaching? I were not. I've never set a trap in me life!"

"You have," said Mary but with less certainty. "You must have done. You set a trap on the moors. My dog, Jemima, found it."

"Jemima?" Dickon raised his eyebrows. "If you're meaning the brown dog that hangs around these grounds, I'm not sure it'll be too fond of that name, seeing as it's a boy."

"A boy?" echoed Mary in astonishment. "Jemima's a boy dog?"

Dickon nodded.

"Oh." Mary chewed her lip for a moment. Whether Jemima was a boy or a girl didn't seem so important right then. She—or he—was hurt and it seemed that Dickon hadn't been responsible for the trap. "Well, that doesn't matter. Not really. What's important is that he's hurt."

"Hurt?" Dickon's voice changed in an instant. "Where is he? Can you take me to him?"

"I could." Mary gave him a wary look. "But why should I trust you?"

"I know how to make him better," said Dickon simply. "Trust that."

Mary met his dark brown eyes and saw the honesty there. "Very well, but if I'm going to show you, I need you to agree to keep a secret."

Dickon nodded and spat on his hand. "On me honor I'll keep it," he said gravely and held his hand out.

Mary was puzzled. "Why have you just spat on yourself?"

Dickon looked surprised. "You spit too," he explained. "Then we shake. Then we're bonded. But if you're too much of a fine lady . . ."

Mary tossed her head. "I am no lady, sir!" she declared. She spat on her hand and shook his firmly. She gave him an impish grin, and he grinned back.

"Now, where's this dog?"

Mary took Dickon to the wall. "We have to climb over here," she said. "We can use the branches of this tree." She pulled herself up.

Dickon followed her, and as they reached the top, a look of delight crossed his face as he gazed at the secret garden spread out on the other side.

Mary's heart swelled with happiness at being able to share her find. "This is my secret," she said, "and you are to keep it. You're just here to help Jem—the dog."

Dickon nodded, and they climbed down, using the creepers. Mary was careful to hang on tight to the leaves so she didn't fall like the day before. When she reached the bottom, she raced away with a whoop. "This way!"

Dickon followed her. They charged through the trees together until they burst into a clearing, and Mary stopped to grab a breath.

"Look at this place," said Dickon, turning around in delight. "There's a badger's sett." He pointed to a bank with a large hole in it. "And when the spring comes there'll be rabbits and squirrels, hedgehogs, stoats, and voles. Foxes too!"

His eyes shone, and Mary loved seeing the excitement on his face. She couldn't wait to show him the rest of the garden, but first she had to find the dog.

"Jemima!" she called. She gave Dickon a slightly rueful look. "I suppose I'll have to change his name."

"Let's get him mended first," said Dickon.

"Jemima!" Mary called again. She sat down and took a piece of Spam out of one of her sandwiches and threw it on the ground.

There was a sudden rustle, and the dog appeared on three legs from a nearby bush. He grabbed the Spam and looked warily at Dickon.

"Hello, fella," said Dickon.

Mary took out some more Spam, and the dog limped toward her.

"How did you get here? Owner not come back

from the war?" Dickon said softly.

The dog stared at him, still wary.

"I'll do you no harm," said Dickon. He glanced at Mary. "Can you get him to come to you?"

She waved the Spam, and the dog approached her. As he passed Dickon, he grabbed him and turned him upside down.

"What are you doing?" Mary gasped as the dog howled. "Let go of him!"

"Shush now." Dickon started to whisper in the dog's ear. Mary couldn't hear what he said, but the dog slowly relaxed and Dickon investigated the wounded leg. As he touched it with careful fingers, the dog whimpered softly.

"You tricked me!" hissed Mary angrily.

The dog whined.

Dickon's eyes met Mary's. "He trusts you. Will you hold his head?"

Mary crept closer and stroked the dog. "How is he?" she said. "How's his leg?"

"Nothing broken, but it's going rotten and if we don't see to it he'll lose his leg—and, chances are, his life," said Dickon, checking the wound again.

"What can you do?" said Mary anxiously.

"Is there running water near here?"

"Yes, there's a stream," said Mary. "If I can remember how to find it." As she looked around doubtfully, the trees seemed to part slightly and the sun shone down, lighting up a path. Mary blinked. Had that really just happened?

Yes, she thought with absolute certainty. *This garden is magic.*

"It's this way," she said, pointing down the path. "I'm sure."

The path took them all the way through the trees to the clearing with the stream. Dickon strode toward the glittering, running water with the dog in his arms. Shrugging off his bag, he knelt on the bank, and holding the dog near the water, he washed out the wound. The dog whimpered, but seemed to sense that the boy was helping him and didn't try to escape.

"There," said Dickon at last.

Mary had been watching, fascinated.

"In me bag, you'll find a cloth. A knife too. Cut the cloth into pieces so I can bind this up and keep the muck out. Quickly now."

For a moment, Mary bristled at being bossed around, but then she told herself not to be silly. Dickon was only trying to help, and he knew more than she did about animals and their wounds. She hurried to his bag and found the sheathed knife and the cloth. It was wrapped around a hunk of rough brown bread and crumbly cheese. She put the food on the grass beside his bag.

"I've never used a knife like this before," she said, pulling it from its sheath.

"Then go careful with it," said Dickon. "Or I'll be fixing you up too."

Frowning with concentration, Mary cut the

cloth into strips and handed them to him. "That's really good, that," said Dickon, looking impressed.

Mary felt a warm glow spread through her. She watched as he wound the strips around the dog's leg, bandaging up the nasty wound. When it was finished, the dog licked Dickon's hands and chin gratefully. Dickon chuckled.

"Feel better does it, sir? Now that's enough with you thanking me," he said, gently pushing the dog away. "Let's see you walk, lad."

The dog hobbled a step and then tried to run, but collapsed in the grass with a howl.

"Dickon! You haven't fixed anything! You've made it worse!" cried Mary. She jumped up to go to the dog, but Dickon held her back.

"No. Wait, lass."

The grass shivered, and as they watched, it seemed to grow around the still form of the dog, wrapping him up, covering him like a protective green blanket. The dog fell asleep.

"Just give it time," Dickon said softly. "Both of you. We've done all we can for now."

Mary gazed at the dog. "We're hoping the garden will magic him well?" she said softly.

Dickon nodded. "Come the morning, we'll have an answer." He looked grave. "Let's hope it's the one we want."

"The garden *will* help," Mary said firmly.

"We'll see," said Dickon.

Getting to his feet, he fetched his bread and cheese. "Now, no point in letting this go to waste," he said. "Do you want some?"

"I have my own sandwiches," said Mary, opening the bag. "I get them from Cook and share them with Jem—the dog."

She took out the sandwiches, and she and Dickon ate in a companionable silence as the grass rustled in the breeze and the sunlight sparkled on the stream.

13

The Hidden Room

That night, Mary returned to Colin's room, wondering what mood she would find him in. To her relief, he seemed happy to see her. "Sit," he said rather grandly, pointing to the end of his bed. "Now I want to know more about this magic garden."

Mary didn't need any more encouragement. She had explored some more with Dickon that afternoon, and she had so much she wanted to tell Colin. "I will, but then you must spit and promise not to breathe a word to anyone. It really is the most wonderful place!" Her eyes shone.

"There are hundreds of trees and plants, the moss glows and there are strange plants that look like giant umbrellas." Her words came faster as she tried to convey the magic of the garden.

"There's an ancient temple that looks as if it's grown up out of the ground, with a lake inside, and a path lined with statues, and a stream that can heal wounds. There are animals there too, most sleeping under the ground still until spring comes, and there are birds. A robin who reveals secrets and a dog who is master of it all!"

"That last bit sounds like rot, but is there really a lake in a temple?" Colin asked eagerly.

"Well, maybe you wouldn't call it a lake," Mary said. "More a pond. But there *is* a stream and I believe it can heal. Now you promised to spit," she reminded him.

Colin shifted in his bed. He spoke awkwardly as if he didn't like admitting he didn't know something. "Mary, you . . . you may need to educate me in how to spit."

Mary laughed and spat on her hand and held it out.

"Oh," Colin said, blinking. "Surprisingly simple." He copied her, and they shook hands.

"Now we have spat and shaken, we can never break the promise," she told him earnestly.

"I won't tell a soul," said Colin. "You have my word. Now I want to know more about this dog. Maybe you will be able to train it," he said. "I have a book on dog training in my bookcase." He pointed across the room. "Fetch it."

Mary laughed. "I most certainly shan't if you talk to me like that." She sat down in the wheelchair instead. "When was the last time you used this chair?"

"Fetch me my book!" Colin said crankily.

She ignored him. "I don't believe your back is half as painful as you make out."

"And I know you didn't kill your mother like you said," retorted Colin. "So who's the bigger liar?"

Mary was shocked. "How do you know that?"

"I said to the maid who cleans my room that I'd heard you moving about, and I demanded she told me who you were. She said you were an orphan and that both your parents died in hospital of cholera. She was very clear you weren't a murderess."

Mary felt a lump swell in her throat. She wished what he said was true, but she knew what she'd done. Not wanting to talk about it, she changed the subject. "Colin, do you trust me? I want to show you something."

"Why would I trust you?" he said.

She raised her eyebrows. He had the grace to look slightly ashamed and nodded. "Very well. But I am not going outside," he added warningly.

"This isn't outside," said Mary. She took the wheelchair over to his bed. "Now shall I help you in?"

"No," he said, his cheeks flushing. "I do not want you to see my back where the hump is growing. Turn away. I can manage on my own."

Mary went over to stand by the door and waited with her back turned to him. She heard him grunting with effort and cursing under his breath, but at long last, he cleared his throat. "You may turn around."

He was sitting in his chair with his dressing gown on over his pajamas. His face was pale.

She hurried behind him, pushing him out into the corridor.

"So I have trusted you tonight," he said, glancing back at her. "I believe you should trust me in return. Tell me why you believe you are a murderess?"

Mary hesitated. She knew how hard it had been for him to agree to leave his bed, and she felt she owed him something in return. "I wished my mother's death," she said in a small voice. "I was angry because she didn't love me, so I wished her dead and then it happened. The cholera came and she and Daddy both died. I am absolutely a murderess, Colin."

"But, Mary, that's—"

"I made it happen," she insisted, glaring at him. She didn't want him trying to make her feel better. She knew it was her fault and that she had to live with the guilt of what she'd done.

He looked alarmed. "Very well," he said hastily. "If you say it is so, then . . . then I believe you." He started to look panicked. "But if you take me to the garden, you will murder me too!"

Mary frowned. "I'm not taking you to the garden. I'm taking you into that room." She pointed to the room with the murals. "There's something you need to see."

She wheeled him inside. He stared at the murals as she found the hidden catch and the door opened into the secret room.

"What is this place?" he said in astonishment as she pushed him into the sparkling room. The radiant moonlight fell on the silvery cobwebs, and the gems on the gowns glittered brightly.

As Colin looked around, his shoulders tensed and his voice rose. "Was this my mother's room? I don't like it here, Mary. Take me back."

"Wait!" said Mary, hurrying over to the pile of photographs. "You need to see these. I was three when your mother died and you and I are about the same age. What do you remember of that time?"

"I don't know and I don't care. Take me back to my room," Colin insisted.

"Colin!" Mary took the box of loose photographs over to him. "Just look at these. Don't be scared," she said as he glanced away. "You'll like them. It's your mother and my mother together. Look."

She showed him the top few photographs and stopped at the one with the two children in it. The boy was slim and dark; the girl was smaller with a chestnut-brown bob. They were holding hands with their mothers.

"It's us," Mary said softly. "It didn't make sense at first because I thought I hadn't been to England before, but now I think my mother must have brought me here when your mother was ill. Martha told me they were very close, so I think she came to see her twin—your mother—one last time before she died. Then afterward she couldn't bear to talk about it and so no one ever mentioned it to me. Isn't it incredible, Colin, that we met when we were young although neither of us can remember it? And look. I think we were inside the secret garden!"

Colin's hand had started to shake. He pushed the picture away. "I don't want to see," he said, his voice trembling with emotion.

"But isn't it extraordinary?" said Mary, her eyes shining as she rushed on. "And do you know what's even more extraordinary? You're walking in the picture, Colin. You don't have a wheelchair or a hump and you don't look ill. Colin, look . . ."

"No!" Colin exclaimed, shoving at her with both hands as she tried to put the photo back in his lap. "No. No. No! I said I don't want to see. You're just doing this to hurt me. You're just jealous because my mother loved me and yours didn't love you!"

Anger rushed through Mary, and she moved to

slap him. She stopped herself at the last moment, but he had started to scream. Desperately scared they would be overheard, she clapped her hand over his mouth to silence him. As they grappled with each other, Colin lost his balance and toppled forward out of his chair, pulling Mary down with him and knocking over one of the dummies on the way. It crashed into the one next to it, and they both fell over, spilling clothes everywhere.

Mary sat up in a daze, and for a moment thought she saw the hazy figures of her mother and Grace bending over Colin in concern. Mary gasped, and the ghosts vanished.

"Colin?" Mary's voice was little more than a squeak. Colin was lying on the floor, very still, his face white, his eyes shut. She crawled over to him. "Colin, are you all right? Colin?"

His eyes opened. Relief overwhelmed her. For a second, she'd thought she had killed him! She knelt beside him and helped him sit up. "Where does it hurt? Where—" She broke off as she realized something. "Your back, Colin!" She looked closely. "You haven't got a hump. Your back is just the same as mine."

"Of course it's not," said Colin angrily.

"It is," Mary insisted. She pulled his pajama top up and ran her hand over his back. "I swear on your mother's life that I can't see a hump there at all. There's absolutely nothing wrong with your spine."

He stared at her, his eyes disbelieving. "But my father said . . ." His voice trailed off. "No. My back is the reason why he makes me have my medicine, the medicine that burns and hurts," he said. "It doesn't make sense if I don't have a hump."

Mary stared at him wordlessly. He was right: it didn't make any sense at all.

Turning it over in her mind, she began to

silently help him back into his wheelchair. His back might appear normal, but his legs certainly didn't seem able to take his weight. It was tricky to get him up.

"Be careful," he said as she struggled to lift him.

"You're telling *me* to be careful?" said Mary with a grin as she managed to maneuver him back into the seat.

Slightly breathless, they looked around the room and then back at each other. They shared a smile.

"I'm sorry," Mary said, really meaning it. "I didn't realize that bringing you here would upset you so much."

"It's hard," Colin admitted. "Seeing all my mother's belongings."

Mary gave her cousin a sideways look. "I . . . I saw your mother and mine," she admitted. His eyes shot to hers. "Just now, when you fell. They were leaning over you as you lay on the floor. I think I've seen their ghosts before. I thought I was imagining it, but now I'm sure I'm not." She shot him a warning look. "If you tell me I'm lying—"

"I won't," he interrupted. "Because I don't think you are. I've . . . I've never told anyone this, Mary, but when the soldiers were here, and I could hear them crying out, I used to see my mother's ghost. She would appear and stand beside me. I always felt she came to comfort me because she knew I was scared."

"And now my mother has joined her," said Mary wonderingly.

Colin hesitated and took hold of her hand, and they glanced around the secret room together. A room full of memories. Memories of twins who had meant the world to each other and memories of a house that had once been very different.

Filled with light, laughter, happiness, Mary thought,

remembering Martha's words. *And now it's just a prison filled with secrets.*

As she spoke, a cloud passed over the moon, and Mary saw the ghostly figures of her mother and aunt standing at the window together, gazing out in the direction of the garden. They turned and looked at her with a wordless appeal in their eyes. This time she felt no fear, just curiosity. "What do you want?" she whispered to them. "What do you want me to do?"

And then the moon shone out again and the figures vanished, leaving just pale silver moonbeams tracing across the clothes on the floor.

14

The Robin's Secret

When Mary was heading outside the next day, she passed the library and saw her uncle in front of the paintings of his wife. His face was rigid.

"No point keeping them," she heard him mutter.

Mary crept past, but as she slipped outside, she thought about her uncle. He was a very strange man. Why didn't he want to keep the pictures of his wife, and why did he keep Colin locked away, not letting him outside, and why did he tell him he had a hunchback?

Does he hate Colin? she wondered. *After all, he didn't go to him when he was sobbing with pain and he makes him take the medicine that he hates.*

But even as the thoughts crossed her mind, Mary remembered the expression on her uncle's face as he had hesitated outside Colin's door. He had looked tortured. She shook her head. Why would her uncle look like that, but not go in to try to comfort Colin? It just didn't make sense. *This house has too many secrets,* she thought.

Glancing back, she caught sight of Mrs. Medlock watching her from an open first-floor window.

Mary carried on, and after a few minutes, she saw Mrs. Medlock come out of the house. Mary smiled to herself and skipped into some nearby trees. Hidden from sight, she ran to an old yew tree and climbed high into its branches. She waited. Sure enough, Mrs. Medlock came hurrying along the path, looking left and right.

So it looks like you're spying on me, Mary thought. *Whatever for?*

She waited until the housekeeper had disappeared from view and then dropped down lightly and doubled back through the trees, heading straight for the wall. She was desperate to get to the garden. She wanted to know how the dog was. Would he be better—or worse?

As she scrambled over the wall, Mary wondered whether there was a gate or door that led into the garden. Surely there must be a way in that didn't involve climbing?

I must try to find the real entrance, she thought.

She climbed down, wondering if Dickon would be there. Hurrying across the carpet of dry leaves, she noticed new green ones unfurling on the branches in the sunshine, and her heart lifted. Spring was approaching, and the garden seemed to be coming back to life.

I could do some weeding, she thought as the magic seemed to guide her feet into the garden of statues. *I could tame some of the undergrowth. Make the flower beds look like they did in the photograph of when I was little.*

She skipped in happiness at the thought and then spotted Dickon in the temple. He had shrugged off his thick winter jacket and was clearing some brambles with his knife. Dickon had taught Mary to whistle the day before, and now she whistled to him. Dickon looked around and lifted his hand in greeting.

"Have you seen him?" Mary asked anxiously, running over. "Is he healing? Is he . . . is he worse?"

There was a rustle, and the dog ran out from the bushes behind Dickon. With a welcoming

Do you want to hear a story?

Mary Lennox roams the forests of her uncle's vast Yorkshire estate alone. That is, until she meets a new friend.

Mary explores Misselthwaite Manor's mysterious surroundings. She stumbles upon an enchanted place, unlike any Mary has ever seen.

Climbing over an ivy-covered wall, Mary discovers a magical garden. Mary must keep this place a secret.

A bright-eyed robin guides Mary to a hidden key that can unlock the gates to the garden!

Archibald Craven

Misselthwaite Manor is owned by Mary's uncle, Archibald Craven. Overcome with grief due to his wife's passing, he has no time for his niece.

Colin Craven

Archibald's son, Colin, is Mary's cousin. Bedridden with a mysterious illness, Colin never leaves his room.

Mrs. Medlock

The manor is run by this stern housekeeper. Always suspicious, Mrs. Medlock takes an instant dislike to Mary.

Martha Sowerby

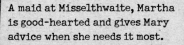

A maid at Misselthwaite, Martha is good-hearted and gives Mary advice when she needs it most.

Dickon meets Mary and a friendship blossoms. With his help, and the magic of the garden, he and Mary heal Hector's injured paw.

Wonderous flowers bloom to life, reaching their leaves and petals out to Mary and Dickon as they run through the secret garden.

Mary is determined to get Colin to the secret garden so he can experience its power for himself. She wonders if the bubbling waters within the garden will heal her cousin, just like it healed Hector.

Mary and Dickon sneak Colin to the garden's stream, where they dip him in the cool, majestic waters.

The power of the garden heals Colin! Standing on his own, he asks to see his father.

Archibald is astonished to see his wife's garden bursting with life and love. It is here that a father and son are reunited after years of heartbreak.

Through love, a family has formed. The garden has shown Mary, Dickon, Colin, and Hector the power to change lives, including their own.

bark, the dog bounded toward Mary.

"He's better!" Mary cried, dropping to her knees. The dog jumped around her, wagging its tail. She stroked and patted him.

"He's still got a limp," Dickon said, walking over to them. "But the leg is taking his weight now."

"The garden cured him." Mary's eyes shone.

Dickon grinned. "Aye, well, the garden had some help."

"No, Dickon," Mary said earnestly. "This is a magic garden! It can heal people—and dogs." She gazed around with new wonder at the overgrown garden, the temple, and the statues. The dog barked at her again, and she barked back.

"What are you doing?" said Dickon, looking amused.

"I'm a Yorkshire terrier!" giggled Mary.

Dickon chuckled and then barked himself. "Then I'm a Yorkshire terrier too!"

Mary ran around in a circle, barking, and the dog ran and woofed with her. "Come on!" she cried, grabbing Dickon's hand.

"What? Where are we going?"

Mary grinned at him. "Just run!"

She sprinted off, happiness bubbling through her as she ran for the sheer joy of it. The dog raced beside her, and she could hear Dickon's boots thudding on the grass behind them. As they charged through the garden, new stems seemed to rise up from the ground, twisting up around the temple columns, buds bursting open into bright red and yellow flowers as the garden responded to their joy.

Sunlight fell on Mary's face, and she opened her arms wide, touching the plants as she ran. Spring had quickly come to her garden, and all around her, the plants were suddenly beginning to bloom. Blue forget-me-nots, tall orange lupins, and red azaleas burst into life. Deep pink and purple flowers appeared on the dark green rhododendron bushes, and white flowers exploded on the twisted branches of a magnolia tree. The buds seemed to open as the children touched them.

"This garden *is* magic, Dickon! I know it is!" Mary cried.

They raced through the giant ferns and reached the stream. They splashed through the temple and ran on. When they could run no longer, they threw themselves down in the long grass near the broken statue where Mary had found the key. The dog lay panting between them. Mary gazed at the cornflower-blue sky. Her blood felt like it was buzzing. Hearing a merry twittering, she saw the robin circling over her. As she propped herself up on her arms, it landed on her knee and then hopped onto her hand. Mary lifted it up carefully. "Hello."

It chirruped as if trying to tell her something important.

Dickon smiled. "You've got a friend there."

"I've met him before," said Mary. She looked at the robin intently. "You showed me where the key was. Are you trying to tell me something else now?"

The robin sang louder.

Mary frowned. What could the robin want her to do? An answer came into her head, and she reached into her pocket with her other hand and pulled out the key. The robin twittered and hopped up and down. "I think he's telling me to find the gate to the garden—the gate this key unlocks."

A sudden wind blew around the garden. "See!" Mary said in delight. "Even the garden agrees with me!"

The robin flew up into the air and circled around before flying to a different statue and perching on it. "We need to follow him!" Mary declared.

Dickon gave a shrug but let her lead the way.

The robin flew back to the wall where Mary had first climbed over.

"Maybe we have to look for the door from the other side," said Mary. "Yes," she decided. "I think that's what he's saying."

Dickon shrugged but seemed happy to follow. They climbed the wall and began to explore it from the other side. As they walked together, with the robin flying ahead of them and the dog at their feet, Mary decided to tell Dickon the story of Rama and Sita and the monkey god, Hanuman. Dickon listened, nodding occasionally.

"Well?" Mary said eagerly when she reached the end. "Did you like the story, Dickon?"

"I liked the idea of a flying monkey," said Dickon.

Mary grinned. Just then, the robin flew to the wall and clung to the curtain of creepers, singing loudly. A gust of wind rushed by, lifting up the ivy and revealing a metal gate underneath.

"Dickon!" gasped Mary, starting to push through the bracken that blocked the way. "It's a gate! A gate to the garden!"

Mary began to pull the creepers away. Dickon joined her, tugging them to one side until they could see the gate beneath. Taking out the key, Mary pushed it into the lock. It stuck for a moment but then moved with a click. Mary turned the handle, and the gate opened. She looked at Dickon in delight. "This is the proper way in. It's what the robin wanted us to find."

The robin circled around her head, tweeting happily.

Mary felt excitement buzzing through her. Already an exciting plan was forming in her mind.

The gateway was wide enough for a wheelchair to fit through. Yes, she knew Colin said he hated the outdoors and it was dangerous to him, but she was sure that wasn't true. If she could just bring him to the garden, maybe he would start to feel better. Maybe . . . just maybe . . . its magic would help heal him like it had helped the dog.

"Oh, Dickon," she breathed, her eyes shining. "Finding this gate could be the thing that really makes all the difference!"

15

Taking Risks

Mary told Dickon her plan, and they hurried to the house. Sneaking in through the back door, they crept up the staircases and along the corridors. Mary knew her plan was dangerous, and she had no idea if Colin would even agree to it, but she also knew she had to try.

As they reached the part of the house where Colin's room was, they became even more cautious.

Mary ran to the end of a corridor, checked the next one, then signaled to Dickon to move. He raced past her and dived into another doorway. Peering out, he beckoned to her, and she made the next move. Corridor after corridor they negotiated their way as they gradually got closer to Colin's room. They were almost there when Mary heard a door handle turning. She threw her arm up to warn Dickon, and they flung themselves into an empty room, hardly daring to breathe. Risking a peek, Mary saw Mrs. Medlock come out of a room and march away without realizing they were there.

They waited a few moments and then made the final dash to Colin's room. His door was locked.

"Who's there?" she heard Colin demand as she rattled the handle. "It's the girl, isn't it?"

"My name is Mary, and you jolly well know it!" she hissed.

"I don't want you here!" said Colin, his voice

rising. "I don't want to see you. You're cruel."

Mary felt like stamping in frustration. "We're past this, Colin. You'll scream. I'll scream. No good will come of it!"

Colin started to yell. There was the sound of running footsteps on the staircase at the end of the corridor. Mary hastily pulled Dickon into the nearest doorway and tried the handle, but it was locked.

She thought they were about to be caught by Mrs. Medlock, but it was Martha who appeared at the top of the staircase. Spotting Mary and Dickon, her mouth dropped open.

"What are you doing here?" she hissed.

"I know about Colin," Mary said quickly. "We're friends."

Martha blinked in astonishment, and then her eyes flicked back to Dickon. "If they catch you here, they'll have you whipped," she said urgently.

"We want to help Colin, Martha. It's worth the risk," Mary said, and to her delight, Dickon nodded.

Martha frowned at her. "You risk being sent to school, miss. We risk more—far more. If Dickon gets discovered here, we'll be turned out and I'll lose all my wages. We'll starve!"

There was the sound of more footsteps. "What's going on?" called Mrs. Medlock's voice. She appeared at the far end of the corridor just as Mary and Dickon ducked back into their doorway and pressed themselves against the heavy door.

Martha hesitated and then walked toward the housekeeper, positioning her body to block Dickon and Mary from sight. "Don't worry yourself, Mrs. Medlock. It's just the young master. I'll deal with him."

"He never normally causes bother at this hour," said Mrs. Medlock, frowning.

"I'll take care of him," Martha said briskly.

"You continue with your chores, if you want."

Mrs. Medlock nodded gratefully. "Very well. Thank you, Martha. There is such a lot to do." She hurried away.

The breath rushed out of Mary, and she saw Martha's shoulders sag too.

"I need to see my cousin, Martha," Mary pleaded, knowing there was no time to waste. Mrs. Medlock could come back any minute. "I think I know a way to help him—to make him feel better."

Martha looked at her uncertainly.

"Please, Martha!" Mary begged.

Martha hesitated and then unlocked the door. Seeing Mary, Colin opened his mouth to scream.

"Do that and you'll never see me again!" Mary said hotly. "It's your decision."

He saw her angry eyes and shut his mouth.

"Now I want you to meet someone," said Mary, her voice softening. She gestured to Dickon to come in. He stepped forward reluctantly. "This is Dickon."

"Hello," said Dickon awkwardly.

Colin looked Dickon up and down. "He's handsome."

"He can whistle," Mary said proudly. "And all animals are his friends." She glanced at Martha, who was watching, wide-eyed. "When's the next time they'll check on my cousin, Martha?"

"About four o'clock," Martha replied. She saw Mary look at the chair. "What are you planning, miss?" she said anxiously.

Mary didn't reply. "He'll be back by four," she said firmly.

"Oh, no. I'm not going anywhere with you," said Colin, starting to shake his head.

Martha looked at Dickon. "You understand what you risk?"

He nodded. "Aye."

Martha bit her lip and then reluctantly left.

"You're coming with us," Mary told Colin. "Dickon and I are going to take you to the secret garden."

Colin looked alarmed. "You want to take me outside? No, I won't go. I won't!"

"When we tried to fix the dog, he refused us too," said Mary, her eyes glinting. "Take his arms, Dickon, and I'll take his legs and we'll carry him down there." Colin screamed. Mary's hand covered his mouth in an instant. "Or you could let us help you into your chair and get you down safely. I promise we won't kill you."

"You can't promise anything of the kind!" Colin said in a panicked voice. "I've told you—my legs don't work and I'm allergic! The pollen, the flowers . . ."

"The flowers won't kill you and if you don't come with us you'll die in this bed and all you'll have seen your whole life will be this wallpaper. Is that what you want?" Mary's voice rose. "Is it?"

"No," he muttered.

Mary's voice softened. "Then let us take you to the garden, Colin. Please?"

16

New Friends

Trying to get Colin out of the house in his wheelchair was very risky. They almost bumped into Mrs. Medlock in one corridor and Mr. Craven in another. Even Mrs. Pitcher almost caught them! However, they managed to hide just in time and not be spotted. It was as though the house itself was helping them. They used the lift to get Colin down to the ground floor and then wheeled his chair out through one of the back doors. Mary pushed Colin across the lawn, hoping Mrs. Medlock wasn't looking out of a window.

"Ow! Ouch!" Colin exclaimed, grabbing the arms of the chair as it bounced across the ruts. "You're going too fast, Mary!"

She ignored him. She had helped him into a warm dressing gown, wrapped a scarf around his neck, and put a hat on his head and a blanket over his legs. She didn't believe the outside would kill him, but she didn't want him catching a chill.

As they hurried into the safety of the trees and Mary stopped to catch her breath, Colin started to cough and clutch his chest. "It's the pollen! I told you. It will kill me!" he gasped.

"Colin!" Mary faced him sternly. "Take a breath."

Colin did as she said.

"Still alive?" questioned Mary.

He gave a tiny nod.

"Pollen won't kill you," she told him firmly. "You may have hay fever and that might make you want to sneeze or feel a bit breathless, but that's all. When we're in a safer place, we'll work out what hurts and what doesn't, but for now you have to try, just as I do, not to fuss. Does that sound fair?"

He looked at her mutinously but nodded again.

"Good. Then let's carry on. We can go more slowly now we're out of sight of the house."

They continued on toward the garden. As they drew near, Mary handed Dickon the key. He went on ahead of her to open the gate.

Reaching the wall with its covering of ivy, Mary paused and said to Colin, "I need you to hold tight now."

"Why?" Colin said suspiciously.

In reply, Mary started to push the chair as hard and fast as she could, aiming straight for the curtain of ivy, building up speed to get over the bracken.

"Mary!" Colin shouted in alarm. "Stop! The wall! The wall!" He screamed and covered his head with his arms, bracing himself for a crash, but suddenly the gate opened. They burst through the ivy curtain, past Dickon, and into the garden.

Mary grinned and slowed down. Over their heads there was a broad canopy of bright yellow laburnum flowers forming a long tunnel that seemed to stretch on and on. The light reflected off the flowers, casting a golden glow on their faces. Colin looked around in wonder as Mary wheeled him through the laburnum tunnel and into the garden. It spread out in front of them, a wonderful secret kingdom.

"See," she said happily to him as he gazed in amazement. "Magic is on our side."

The robin circled around Colin's head, singing joyfully.

"Well?" Mary said.

"It . . . it's . . ." Colin stared around, lost for words.

Mary felt a rush of happiness at the incredulity on her cousin's face. "I know," she said, not needing him to say any more. "Come and see. There's so much to show you!"

She wheeled him through the garden, showing him the statues and the flower beds bright with spring crocuses and daffodils that had pushed their way up through the weeds. Mary and Dickon took him to the grove of giant, umbrella-like plants and into the ruined temple with its glittering pool.

"I want to leave my chair and feel the grass," Colin said, and so they helped him out and he sat in the soft grass, leaning his back against one of the temple pillars while Dickon picked up his gardening fork again and Mary used a trowel to dig out the weeds in the flower beds. As they worked, Colin started to ask Dickon the names of the different flowers.

"What do you call this one?"

"That's a hydrangea," Dickon replied.

"And this?" questioned Colin, pointing to a yellow flower.

"Hypericum," said Dickon.

"Hypericum," Colin repeated slowly.

Just then, Mary heard a rustle in a nearby bush. "Colin. There's a good friend I would like you to meet," she said. Reaching into her pocket, she took out some Spam and gave it to him. "Hold it out and he'll come."

"He's here?" breathed Colin. "The dog?"

"Just hold it out. He wants to say hello. I can tell," Mary said.

Colin held out the meat, and the dog trotted out from behind the bush. Colin watched, fascinated, as the dog approached him. It looked at him for a moment and then quickly took the Spam from his hand.

Colin yelped in surprise and delight. "He took it from me!"

"He did," said Mary, grinning.

The dog sat down beside Colin and licked his fingers. "Now he's licking me!" Colin said, half-alarmed, half-delighted.

"He does that," said Mary, glancing at Dickon, who smiled.

"It tickles," said Colin. Suddenly he pulled his hand back and looked doubtful. "He's not diseased, is he?"

"Not that we've seen," said Dickon.

Colin relaxed and stroked the dog's ears. "What's his name?"

"He was called Jemima," said Dickon with a sly glance at Mary. "Till *she* knew different."

Mary didn't mind being teased. "I didn't know he was a boy at first," she protested. "We haven't thought of a new name for him yet, Colin. He's just called . . . dog."

"He needs a better name than that," said Colin. "Perhaps we should call him . . ." He frowned. "Oh, I don't know. What was your father called, Mary?"

"Marcus," said Mary uncomfortably. "But can we not name him that?"

"Well, we shouldn't name him after my father either," said Colin. "I can't believe he's been keeping me in my room all this time when the outside clearly doesn't hurt me. What about you, Dickon? What's your father called?"

"Hector," said Dickon, looking down. "He was a brave man."

Mary and Colin both stared at him. "Was—you mean he's dead?" Mary questioned.

Dickon nodded briefly.

"Would you mind if we named the dog after him?" Mary said.

Dickon shook his head and smiled.

"Well, that's settled, then," Colin said.

The dog lay down beside him, and he put a hand on its head. "Dog, you are now called Hector," he said solemnly. "Mary you already know—and Dickon too. Well, I am Colin, your new friend."

The dog barked as if he understood. Mary, Dickon, and Colin all laughed and barked back at him. The sunshine caught the embroidered butterflies on Mary's dress, and for a moment they seemed to actually flutter their wings and fly around her before landing back in the pattern again.

Seeing the happiness on her cousin's face, Mary

felt as if her heart was swelling like a balloon that was being blown up. *Yes,* she thought, remembering Martha's earlier words. *This was definitely worth the risk.*

Overhead the robin twittered as if it agreed.

17
Caught!

Mary and Dickon managed to get Colin safely back into the house by four, and Mary headed to the garden once more. She was walking through a tunnel of yew trees, when she heard a twig crack behind her. Glancing around, she caught sight of Mrs. Medlock ducking behind a trunk. Mary smiled to herself and, diving to one side, began to run through the trees. She heard Mrs. Medlock's exclamation and ran faster. Once she was out of her sight, Mary scrambled up a nearby fir and sat in the branches as quiet as a dormouse.

A few minutes later, Mrs. Medlock came puffing up. She stopped and looked around, clearly exasperated. As she turned to go back to the house, Mary dropped a fir cone on her head. It bounced off her gray hair, and Mary had to stifle a giggle.

When Mrs. Medlock had gone, Mary jumped down and carried happily on her way. She took the key out of her pocket and headed for the gate. But just before she reached it, Mrs. Medlock stepped out of the shadow of the trees and grabbed her arm. "You think you can just sneak around and act how you like, don't you, girl?" she said angrily.

"Wh-what?" stammered Mary, completely taken aback.

"Little savage," hissed Mrs. Medlock. "I knew

you were hiding something!"

The key, Mary thought. She managed to slip it into her pocket. "I don't know what you mean—"

"You and your secret ways," Mrs. Medlock interrupted. "Poking about. Sneaking off." Her fingers gripped Mary's arm tightly.

Mary began to feel afraid. Mrs. Medlock looked almost insane. "Mrs. Medlock, whatever you think I've been doing, I promise . . ."

"You're nothing but a common little thief!" Mrs. Medlock snapped.

Mary was so shocked she didn't know what to say. Whatever did Mrs. Medlock mean? She'd never stolen anything in her life!

"After the master was good enough to take you in—this is how you repay him!" Mrs. Medlock said. She reached into her pocket and pulled out a string of pearls. Mary's heart dropped. The pearls! She'd meant to put them back in the secret room, but she'd forgotten.

"I . . . I . . ." she stammered. "I didn't mean to take them."

Mrs. Medlock glared at her furiously. "The master is waiting!" she snapped.

Mary was marched to the house, her mind racing. She had to make her uncle believe she had never intended to keep the pearls. Surely he would listen and understand? But as Mrs. Medlock pulled her up the stone steps and into the entrance hall, she saw her uncle standing on the staircase, and his face was terrible. Fury flashed in his eyes.

"So you found her, Mrs. Medlock?"

Mrs. Medlock gave a triumphant nod. "Messing around on the grounds. Look at the state of her."

"Bring her upstairs," ordered Mr. Craven, setting off up the staircase.

"Uncle . . . sir." Mary tried to tear her arm away from Mrs. Medlock, but the housekeeper's fingers gripped tightly. "I didn't mean to take the pearls. I was going to put them back."

"Where did you find them?" he demanded.

Mary hesitated. She had a feeling that if she said she had been in Aunt Grace's room that would get her in even more trouble. "Under a floorboard," she lied.

"Which floorboard?"

"I . . . I can't remember." Tears prickled Mary's eyes. "I'm sorry."

"You understand these pearls mean something to me?" her uncle barked.

Mary nodded unhappily.

"She's been everywhere, sir," broke in Mrs. Medlock. "To the boy too. When I went into his room this morning, his chair had moved. It was that that aroused my suspicions, and so I checked her room and discovered the pearls."

"My son? She's found my son?" His eyes bored

into Mrs. Medlock, Mary temporarily forgotten. "Have we just given her full run of the house, Mrs. Medlock?" he said incredulously.

"I warned you, sir, what a young girl could be like. Yes, I did," Mrs. Medlock said.

Mr. Craven looked back at Mary. "Was it not explained to you that you were to stay away from the parts of the house that were not yours to roam in?"

"Colin is my friend. . . ." Mary's voice faltered. "I just thought . . . if I could excite him about life then . . . then . . ."

"You stupid child!" exclaimed her uncle. "He is weak. Your excitement could kill him!"

"I . . . I didn't know. I was just trying to make things better." Mary realized they were heading toward Aunt Grace's room. Her heart started to pound. "Where are you taking me?"

Her uncle pulled her into the room with the

murals and glanced back at her. "I shall give you one last chance, Mary, and this time I suggest you answer truthfully. Where did you find"—his mouth tightened—"my wife's pearls?"

Mary didn't know what to say.

"There is only one place they would have been," Mr. Craven continued. He opened the secret door, revealing the hidden room. The two dummies were still lying on their side, the clothes scattered over the floor.

"Oh, girl, what have you done?" whispered Mrs. Medlock in horror as they surveyed the chaos.

"I'm sorry!" cried Mary, seeing the pain leap into her uncle's eyes as he looked at the mess. He walked slowly forward without speaking and picked up one of the dummies, straightening the dress on it. His hands lingered on the silky fabric, and then he shut his eyes as if his loss was suddenly too much to bear.

Tears spilled down Mary's cheeks. She had never meant to hurt him.

He swallowed and turned, his face now set like stone. "Mrs. Medlock, look into finding a school for my niece."

Mary stepped toward him. "No, I didn't mean any harm!" she pleaded. "Please."

Her uncle ignored her. "Find somewhere to educate some civility in her," he said coldly. "In the meantime, I do not wish to see or hear her. Do I make myself clear, Mrs. Medlock?"

"Yes, sir." Mrs. Medlock nodded.

As Mary was pulled away, she glanced back and saw her uncle sinking down among the dresses on the floor. He looked broken and completely alone.

18

Prisoner!

Mrs. Medlock pushed Mary into her bed-room, and Mary heard the key turn. She tugged frantically at the door handle, but she was locked in.

"Open this door!" she shouted.

"If you need the bathroom in the night, you'll see we've put a chamber pot under your bed," Mrs. Medlock said through the door. "Martha will let you out in the morning."

Mary heard Mrs. Medlock walking away down the corridor. "Let me out!" she cried, rattling the handle. "I didn't mean to hurt anyone. I just wanted to help." Anger erupted inside her. "I know you're enjoying this!" she yelled. "I know you are! But I won't be sent away again—I won't!"

In a rage, she ran to the rocking horse and pushed it hard, ramming it into the door. It smashed into the wood and overturned. As it banged down, a secret hatch in its belly opened and papers spilled out.

Mary gasped, her rage disappearing with her shock. She crouched down and picked the papers up. They were letters. And they were in her mother's handwriting. . . .

My dearest Grace, they all began.

Mary leafed through them. As her eyes raced over the words, she realized they were all from her mother to her aunt. But why had they been hidden away? As she read some of the passages, she began to understand. The letters were between two sisters who kept no secrets from each other. They talked about their lives, their children, their husbands, in a way that they would not have wanted anyone else to see. Mary skipped over the bits about life in India, about her and her father, her eyes seeking out the passages where her mother talked about Grace's illness, Colin, Archie . . . It was strange to imagine her forbidding uncle ever being called by such an informal name.

Outside, the sky darkened, the sun set, and the moon rose. Mary turned on her bedside lamp and carried on reading the letters in bed, putting things together, starting to make sense of some of the mysteries that surrounded her. She only looked up from them when she heard faint screams. She swallowed, her fingers tightening on the letter she was holding. *Colin.* He would be wondering why she didn't go to visit him as usual. She glared at the locked door, longing to get out.

Mary fell asleep fully clothed. She only woke in the morning when Martha came in with a tray. Mary hastily shoved the letters under her bedcovers. To her relief, Martha was too busy looking at the overturned rocking horse to notice.

"What's been going on here, then?" she said. Not waiting for an answer, she heaved the horse up and pushed it back into its place. "Mrs. Medlock's in a right rage with you," she said to Mary. "There's just stale bread for breakfast, no porridge."

"I don't care," said Mary defiantly. "How long is she planning on keeping me prisoner?"

Martha's mouth twitched. "Hark at you. You're no prisoner. I'm to leave your room unlocked when I've finished, but if I were you, I'd stay out of everyone's way."

Mary felt a rush of relief. She could leave her

room and go to the garden. She could see Colin and Dickon. She jumped up and hugged Martha.

Martha gasped in surprise. "Let me go, miss— you're fair squeezing me to death!" But as Mary drew back, she saw the smile on Martha's face.

"I'll make my bed," Mary said hastily as Martha went over to the rumpled sheets.

"You can't do that, miss," Martha protested.

"Oh, yes I can." Mary pushed Martha toward the door. "In fact, I order you to leave it." She smiled. "You can go now."

Shaking her head as if she didn't know what to make of her, Martha left.

Mary gathered up the letters and put them into her bag. Then she got changed and made as good an attempt as she could to make her bed, not wanting Martha to get into trouble. She smoothed the sheets and then set off. She needed to go to the garden and find out if a suspicion the letters had put in her mind was true. If it was, then maybe she had discovered where the magic of the garden came from!

Mary slipped out of the house and headed across the lawn. She ran toward the trees and found the gate. Pulling the curtain of creepers back, she went straight into the part of the garden with the statues and flower beds. Dickon was there already, his coat off, humming a song. He had some gardening tools with him, and he was digging up the weeds near the temple at the far end. The robin was perched on the handle of a gardening fork that was dug into the ground, and the dog was snuffling near Dickon's feet. The plants around him were a riot of spring color—reds, oranges, pinks, purples, blues.

The dog spotted Mary as she approached and ran over to say hello.

"Morning," called Dickon.

"Morning!" gasped Mary, running past them.

"Hey, where are you going?" Dickon called.

"Follow me!" she cried.

The robin circled around her head. She let it lead her through the garden, trusting that the magic would help it to know where she needed to go. It took her through the giant ferns and into thick trees. The bushes seemed to close in on her, the vines snaking at her ankles, branches blocking her path as if the garden didn't want her to go that way, but she forced her way through, following the robin. It twittered loudly as if it was urging her on. Determination beat through Mary. The garden had yet more secrets to reveal, and she was going to find them out.

She burst into a clearing that she had never been in before. She stopped as she took in the oak tree at the center of it. There was an old swing hanging from a strong branch. The robin landed on the oak tree and sang knowingly at Mary.

"Oh," Mary said softly, realizing she had found what she had been looking for. She walked slowly up to the swing and crouched down beside it. Then she looked back at Dickon, her face serious. "This is the place," she whispered. "The place where everything happened."

Dickon looked confused.

"It's where my aunt came to die," Mary went on.

The robin flew down to land on her shoulder. Dickon came over, approaching her slowly as if she was a wild animal he didn't want to frighten. "What do you mean?"

Mary told him what she had worked out from the letters. "My aunt was very ill with cancer, and my mother came over from India to see her in her last days—she brought me with her, but I don't remember. I was only little." She looked at the swing. "My mother wrote that she wanted to be with my aunt when she died and she knew my aunt wanted to die here in this garden by this tree. It was her special place."

She looked around the clearing. "My aunt made this whole garden. She grew the flowers. She put the statues in place. She designed the temple. After she died, I think my uncle locked the garden up because it caused him too much pain." Her eyes met Dickon's. "I believe my aunt is the reason the garden is magic. I think she wanted me to find the key so"—she took a breath—"so I could use the garden to cure her son."

Mary looked fiercely at Dickon, daring him to laugh. But he didn't.

"I haven't got long," she went on. "They're sending me away to school. I have to see if the garden can heal Colin before I go. But I can't do it on my own, Dickon. I need your help."

He nodded solemnly. "Tell me what you need me to do."

19

Unlocking the Past

If I can help Colin get better, I don't care what happens to me,
Mary thought fiercely as she crept through the
corridors with Dickon behind her. *They can send me to
school and do whatever they like.*

To her relief, through one of the windows, she
saw Mrs. Medlock setting out in the car. At least
that was one less person to avoid!

Colin was waiting for them. "Are we going to

the garden again?" he asked eagerly.

"Yes," Mary told him.

"Why didn't you come and see me last night?" Colin asked her accusingly as they set off down the corridor. "I waited and waited, and you didn't come."

"I couldn't," she said. "I was locked up. They want to send me away to school, Colin!"

"Send you away?" echoed Colin.

She nodded miserably. "Your father is determined. Mrs. Medlock worked out I'd been visiting you, which made him angry, and then they found I'd been in your mother's room. It was in such a mess from the other night."

"I will tell Father I don't want you to go!" declared Colin.

Mary sighed. "I don't think that will work. But let's not talk about this now. Let's just think about the garden."

"Our garden!" Colin said happily.

Mary hesitated. It wasn't their garden—she knew that now—but she wasn't sure he was ready to hear that.

When they reached the garden, she put her plan into action. The stream had cured Hector's leg. Maybe it could do the same for Colin?

At first, Colin didn't like the idea of going in the water. "It looks cold," he said doubtfully as they helped him remove his outer clothes. "I think I shall just sit here on the bank."

"No, you're going in," Mary told him. "You're not to be a baby about this," she said warningly.

He started to frown but then sighed. "Oh, very well," he grumbled.

Mary and Dickon began to lower him gently into the flowing water. Colin gasped. "It *is* cold!" The leaves of the ferns around the stream seemed to shiver in sympathy. "Very, very cold." His eyes widened, and he clutched Mary's arm. "I don't think I can do this."

"Course you can," said Dickon cheerfully.

"No, I don't think so!"

"We've got you," Dickon told him.

Colin looked from Dickon to Mary and then took a breath. "Well," he said bravely as they lowered him a little further, "I suppose it's not so freezing after all."

Soon he was sitting in the stream, the pure, clean water flowing over him with only his shoulders and head above the water. "I've done it!" he exclaimed, his face breaking into a look of delight. "I've actually done it!"

The ferns began to stop shivering as he smiled.

"Now you can learn to float," said Dickon. "Hold your arms out and lie back." Colin hesitated. "Mary and I have you," Dickon said.

Colin did as he was told, leaning back and

turning his face up to the blue sky. As he stretched his arms out to the side, a look of joy crossed his face. Dickon nodded at Mary, and they removed their hands.

"And now you're on your own," said Dickon as they backed quietly away.

Colin grinned and then started to laugh, and as he did so his hands splashed into the water, sending droplets raining over Mary and Dickon. Mary squealed, and Colin laughed even louder.

When he was ready to come out, Mary and Dickon helped him get dressed again, and then they all set to work on the grounds around the temple. Colin was happy to sit on the grass, pulling out the weeds from a patch of bright spring bulbs—daffodils, bluebells, little purple grape hyacinth—while Dickon dug and Mary crouched down, separating out plants that were growing too close together. They worked in companionable silence for a while.

"Done!" Colin declared. "Move me over there now, please!"

Mary and Dickon hoisted him up by his arms and put him down in a new spot. Humming to himself, he carried on with his work. Dickon and Mary smiled at each other.

Looking up, Colin caught the smiles. "What?" he said suspiciously.

"Nothing. We're just enjoying your happiness," said Mary.

"We're all happy, aren't we?" said Colin contentedly.

"True enough," said Dickon, nodding.

"We're pirates!" exclaimed Mary.

"We're lords!" Dickon grinned.

Colin threw his hands dramatically into the air. "We are conquerors of this fair and beautiful land! This is our garden and we love it!"

"No, it's not," said Mary quickly.

Colin frowned. "What?"

"It's not our garden," Mary said. "It's happy we're here, but it was made by someone else and it still belongs to them." She bit her lip and decided it was now or never: she had to tell Colin what she knew. "Come with me. I need to show you something."

Dickon gave her a concerned look. "Mary . . ."

"I have to show him, Dickon," she said. "He needs to see."

"See what?" Colin said warily.

"Come with us," said Mary.

She and Dickon pushed Colin's wheelchair through the temple, past the broken statue, through the grove of umbrella plants and the overgrown trees. The wheelchair bumped and bounced over the tree roots. Colin gripped the sides tightly. He'd fallen silent. Eventually, they reached the clearing with the oak tree and the swing.

As they pushed him into the clearing, Mary felt the air go still as if the garden was holding its breath.

As Colin's eyes fell on the oak tree and the swing, a look of horrified understanding dawned on his face. "Stop! I command you to stop!"

She halted. Colin stared at the swing, his face paler than ever.

"You know what happened here, then?" Mary said softly.

A muscle jumped in Colin's jaw. "They told me my mother died in her favorite clearing, where she used to have a swing. Is this the place?"

Mary nodded.

Colin started to struggle upright, using his arms to push himself up to a standing position. "Why would you bring me here?"

"Because you needed to see it," said Mary,

shocked at the hurt in his eyes.

"Would *you* like to see the place where your mother died?" he cried.

"My mother died in a hospital, alone and in pain!" Mary retorted. "I thought you would like to see that your mother died in a peaceful place, a better place. I thought that it would help!"

Colin sank back into his wheelchair. "Well, you thought wrong," he muttered. There was a long silence. When he spoke, his voice was tight. "Can you fetch me some flowers, please, Dickon? The white ones."

With an anxious look at Mary, Dickon nodded and did as he was asked.

"And then can you take me home?" Colin continued stiffly. "I don't want to be here."

"You don't understand!" said Mary, knowing her plan was going horribly wrong and wanting desperately to make it right. "Colin, your mother didn't want to leave you, but she had no choice. She came here to die because it was beautiful, and I think that, when she died, she made the garden magical. It cured Hector's leg and . . ." She swallowed. "And I believe it could . . ."

"No!" Colin cut in furiously, his knuckles white as he gripped the arms of his chair. "Don't say it. Don't!" he ground out. "I didn't want to see the dresses and I didn't want to see this. I want to go home!"

Mary lapsed into silence as Dickon handed the white flowers to Colin. Without a word, Colin scattered them on the grass, bright splashes of white against the green.

His shoulders slumped. "Take me home, please," he said to Dickon.

"Of course."

Dickon wheeled Colin away. As they headed back through the trees, the plants around Colin's chair seemed to shrink, gunnera and vines curling in on themselves, branches drooping and leaves turning brown with sadness as he passed.

Disappointment crashed over Mary. She didn't know what she'd expected. Maybe that Colin would find some peace in seeing where his mother had died, in knowing that she was still there, in her way, in the garden. Mary hadn't meant to hurt him. She looked around the clearing. What was she going to do now?

"Tell me," she whispered to the garden. "Please show me the way."

Mary couldn't sleep that night. She got up and fetched her mother's letters, then she sat on the floor in her room, looking through them, her mind turning over everything again, trying to work out what to do for the best.

A memory flashed into Mary's mind. Her

father was hugging her, wiping away her tears. *Your mother is sad at the moment, monkey, and her sadness has made her unwell. Don't be angry with her that she doesn't want to see you. It's not her fault. One day you'll understand.*

Do I understand now? Mary thought. She certainly felt like she was beginning to see the past differently.

She looked up and saw her mother standing by the window. Her eyes were full of sadness—sadness, Mary now knew, for the sister she had lost.

Mary was too shocked to speak. A gust of wind rushed through the room. It swept the letters up and sent them swirling high into the air. Mary grabbed them.

"Mummy, I'm sorry," Mary whispered. "I didn't understand. But I think I do now."

Her mother's gaze met hers, and she smiled, then vanished. Mary suddenly knew what she had to do.

In the morning, she went straight to Colin's room with the letters. The door was locked. She rattled the handle.

"It's me. Can you call Martha so she'll let me in?"

"I don't want to see you today," said Colin in a hard voice. "And I don't want to go to the garden."

"But I've got something to show you," Mary pleaded. "I found some letters from my mother to yours. They talk about you and her illness, how Archie—your father—worries about your health so much because of his own hunchback. She says he's scared you'll be a hunchback too and that he's desperate to protect you. She talks about how fearful she is that he'll project his own fears onto you and make you ill after she's gone, which is exactly what he has done. I think you'll like to see them and it may change how you feel. Please?"

There was a silence. Mary waited, wondering what he was going to say, and suddenly the door opened. Her eyes widened in shock. Colin had got out of bed and opened the door himself. He was hanging on to it, standing up but looking shaky.

"I need to read those letters," he said. Then his legs shook, and he collapsed on the floor with a cry. Mary tried to catch him, but she wasn't strong enough and she ended up crashing down with him.

"Ow!" she gasped as they both hit the floor.

He pushed himself off her. "Sorry."

"You walked, Colin!" Mary exclaimed, not caring about her bruises. "You got out of bed and walked!"

He looked at his legs in confusion. "I did, didn't I?"

Mary beamed. "Now will you believe in the magic?"

She helped Colin into his chair and showed him the letters. "Here. Read them," she said, pushing them onto his lap.

He nodded. "I will but not here. In the garden."

They set off. When they reached the garden, they found Dickon trimming the hedges near the statues in the sun. They explained why they had come and then sat down together in the flower-filled clearing by the swing. Colin and Mary read through the letters while Dickon sat nearby, stroking Hector.

"Listen to this, Mary!" said Colin, reading out a passage. *"She's bold, slightly dangerous, and she has a spirit that nothing can quench. I am so very proud of her."*

"Who's she talking about?" said Mary, puzzled.

Dickon chuckled.

"You, you idiot!" Colin grinned. "She's telling my mother about you. She loved you, Mary."

Mary frowned. She'd skipped over the passages

that weren't about Colin and his mother and father. "That can't be right," she said uncertainly. Despite the night before, it was hard to change the thinking of a lifetime. "My mother didn't want me anywhere near her. She certainly wasn't proud of me." But for the first time, the words sounded slightly automatic—as if they were words she was repeating because they were what she always said, rather than words she meant.

She changed the subject. It was Colin who was important. "Look, here's a bit about you. *I'm so pleased Colin is making you laugh so. A whole day pretending to be a dog. What a delight he is! Archie sounds as if he loves him dearly. I'm just as besotted with Mary.*" Her voice slowed as she realized what she had just read out.

"My father doesn't love me," said Colin, shaking his head. "If he loved me, he wouldn't give me medicine I don't need, and keep me shut in my room, and he would come and see me."

Dickon shrugged. "Folk act in strange ways when they're hurting. Just like animals."

Mary thought about when Hector had been injured and had snapped at her because he had been in such incredible pain.

"Loss changes people," Dickon went on. "Why, even your mother, Mary. It's clear from those letters she loved you, even if you think different."

"You don't know what my mother was like," Mary said.

"No." Dickon paused. "But I know what it's like to lose someone."

They were all silent for a few minutes. Colin broke the silence by reading out another passage. "Listen to this: *She reminds me so much of you in the way she looks and the way she acts, Grace. She makes stories up all the time and loves to put on puppet shows. She did one for me the night before last all about an Indian myth. It was a very elaborate affair indeed. Poor Ayah had to make some silk curtains for it! I love to watch her and listen to her tales."*

Mary could hardly believe it. "She wrote she liked my plays?"

Colin nodded. "So are you sure your mother hated you, Mary? Quite sure?" he said, handing her the letter.

Mary reread the words, and as she did so, a light seemed to come on in her head. Memories flashed in front of her eyes, the past twisted and rearranged itself, and suddenly she began to see her childhood in a new way, to tell a different story about her past—the mother who had hated her daughter so much she didn't want to look at her became a mother whose daughter reminded her so much of her dead sister that she couldn't bear to look at her. She was a mother whose grief for her twin sister was so overwhelming that she had shut herself off from the world—a wounded animal, chasing away anyone who tried to come near, even her own child.

She did love me, Mary thought.

"Maybe neither of us know our parents as well as we think," said Colin.

As Mary nodded slowly, she heard the faint sound of laughter and saw the ghostly figures of her mother and aunt, and Colin and herself when they were both little, skipping between the statues, holding each other's hands in a chain. The adults' eyes shone with love as they looked down at their children. Then they danced on toward the temple and dissolved into light.

Mary couldn't stop thinking about the letters for the rest of the day. Not just the passages about her, but the passages about her uncle too. Her aunt made it sound like he had loved Colin very much. So why did Uncle never visit Colin now? And why had he forced Colin to take medicine and let him believe he had a hump? Was Colin's illness really only a result of his father projecting his own fears onto him, just as Aunt Grace had worried he would?

She was settling Colin back in his room later that day, when Martha came hurrying in. "Miss! It's Mrs. Medlock. She's looking for you. She mustn't find you here!"

Mary raced away. She ran down the corridors and emerged on the main staircase to see her uncle come in through the front door. Mary was about to disappear to her room when Mrs. Medlock came out from the ballroom. "There you are, girl. I've been searching high and low."

"I was outside," said Mary, glad she was still wearing her outdoor clothes as proof.

Mrs. Medlock smiled, reminding Mary of a cat that had just seen a bowl of cream. She looked extremely satisfied with herself. Mary felt a shiver of foreboding run down her spine.

"Well, we've had quite the surprise today," Mrs.

Medlock said. "We've just had word from Miss Clawson's Seminary for Young Ladies." Her smile grew even broader. "And they're ready to take you."

"To take me?" echoed Mary, her heart filling with fear.

"Yes." Mrs. Medlock's smile widened trium-phantly. "You're to go to school, girl. We've already packed your possessions. The car will be here to collect you tomorrow afternoon!"

20

A Way Out

Mary stared at Mrs. Medlock in horror. "School! No, I'm not ready! I can't go!"

"You have no say in it, child," Mrs. Medlock said, her eyes glinting victoriously. "It's all arranged. It's a school that is full of the right sort of people—and the right sort of discipline."

Mary saw her uncle walk by below. She flew down the stairs. "Uncle. No!" she appealed.

"Oh, no you don't," gasped Mrs. Medlock, hastening after her. "You leave your uncle alone!"

"Uncle . . . Mr. Craven . . . sir! Please don't send me away. Please! I need to be here!" Mary begged.

Her uncle carried on walking without even looking at her. Fury burst through Mary. Blinded by rage, she grabbed his arm. "Colin doesn't have a hump!" she shouted. "Why do you keep saying he does?"

"What are you talking about now?" her uncle snapped, shaking her off.

"Colin! He doesn't have a hump and you know it!" She took in the astonishment on his face and suddenly realized something. "But of course," she breathed. "You haven't seen his back, have you? You don't visit him enough to know what it's actually like."

"When Colin was younger, the physician said

that he believed that he would develop a hump like mine unless Colin had medicine and followed his orders," Mr. Craven said stiffly. "I have done as he recommended. I do not want my son to suffer as I have suffered. His body is weak."

"But not because he has a hump!" Mary exclaimed. Suddenly she saw the chance to make things better for Colin. "It's only because he's shut up and made to believe he's an invalid and never gets to use his legs. You can change that," Mary said passionately. "He isn't dying. Please! You've got to believe me!"

A puffing Mrs. Medlock had now reached Mary and tried to pull her away. "Stop with your talking or this will get much worse."

But Mary fought her off. She had to make her uncle understand. "This isn't what Aunt Grace would have wanted for Colin," she cried passionately. "Don't you see, Uncle? This isn't what she would have wanted for either of you!"

Mr. Craven erupted. "Silence, child. You know nothing of my wife."

"I'm sorry, sir," Mrs. Medlock gasped. "I shall see that she's punished."

Mary stamped her foot, desperate to make them understand. "I know that she wouldn't have stood outside his door while he cried at night! I know she loved the outdoors and wouldn't have wanted Colin to be shut up inside and told he has a hump on his back when he has none! Can't you see what you're doing? This house has become a prison—for both of you!"

Her uncle gazed at her for a long moment and then strode away.

"I'm sorry, sir. She leaves tomorrow," Mrs. Medlock called after him desperately.

"Good!" Mr. Craven snapped, without glancing back.

Mary was marched to her room by Mrs. Medlock and pushed roughly inside. Forgetting the vow she had made all those months ago to never cry again, she wore herself out with sobbing. She didn't think she could bear to be sent away to school, to leave her friends and the secret garden.

She cried herself to sleep and woke up in the middle of the night. As she opened her eyes, everything came flooding back and a steely determination filled her. They could try to send her away if they wanted, but they'd have to find her first!

She left her bedroom and began to creep downstairs. Her uncle's study door was open. There was a light shining out. Mary stole a quick look inside. Archibald was sitting in a leather chair at a table beside the window. On the table was a bottle of whiskey and in one hand he had a half-filled glass.

In the other, he held a framed photograph. It was the one she had seen in his study before. Aunt Grace was in the front of the picture. She was sitting on the grass and Colin was looking over her shoulder, his little arms around her neck. They were both smiling at the person holding the camera.

Mary saw her uncle dash his hand across his face. "What have I done?" he muttered. "Oh, Grace, what have I done?"

She swallowed and was about to creep past when there was a fizzle and the lights suddenly went out. Mary froze and waited for her eyes to adjust. Using the light from the moon, her uncle fumbled with a candle and some matches. He burned his hand as he tried to light it and exclaimed angrily as the match went out. He tried again, striking another match and then throwing it down when it burned out. Desperately hoping she wouldn't trip over anything or bump into anything, Mary hurried past and ran down the main staircase. She grabbed her warmest coat and boots from the cloakroom and then scurried out through the back door. As the cold night air hit her face, she felt both relieved and scared. She'd done it! She'd escaped!

Mary slept that night in the secret temple with Hector beside her. She woke, feeling hungry, as the sun rose. Dickon came through the gate, whistling. He stopped in surprise when he saw her sitting on the steps with Hector, watching the early morning sunrise, its rays falling on the perfect sea of flowers that now bloomed around the temple and statues. The weeds had been conquered, and the flowers had opened to the sun. Clumps of white lily of the valley and nodding bluebells clustered in the shady areas with tall pink foxgloves behind them. Hydrangea bushes covered with enormous lilac and pink blooms that looked like pom-poms spilled from the borders, along with clouds of white orange blossom and yellow hypericum.

"Mary? What are you doing here?" Dickon asked.

"They are going to send me to school today," she said glumly. "But I won't go. I won't, Dickon!"

He nodded, understanding.

"Colin will be wondering where I am," Mary said anxiously. "Can you go to him? Get Martha to help you and bring him here?"

She watched as he left the garden. What would everyone be doing in the house? They would have realized she had gone by now. What would they be saying? A feeling of satisfaction that she had out-witted Mrs. Medlock filled her, warming her up and making her forget about her cold fingers and toes. As the sun rose higher, she felt its warmth sinking into her skin, and she went to the stream to get some water to drink.

When she came back, she saw Dickon pushing Colin in his chair. Both boys were looking excited and flushed. "We had such a near miss, Mary!" Colin called. "Mrs. Medlock almost caught Dickon in my room. He had to hide in my wardrobe. When she left, he had to push me as fast as he could. I thought he was going to bounce me clean out of my chair." His eyes flew to her face. "What's going on? Dickon said you've run away."

She ran over to him. "I have. I can't go to school, Colin. I just can't!" She looked around the garden. "And I don't need to." A plan had formed in her mind in the night. "I can stay here!" She saw his doubtful look and rushed on. "I'll be happy. You can bring me food and clothes. Blankets too."

Colin shook his head. "I know you don't want to go to school, and we don't want you to go either. . . ." he said slowly.

"He's right, we don't," Dickon put in.

Mary was grateful as she saw the warm friendship in their eyes.

"But you can't stay locked up in this garden,"
Colin went on, pushing himself out of the chair
and standing on shaky legs. "It's as bad as me being
locked up in my room. Life needs living."

"Says the boy who's seen none of it!" retorted
Mary.

"Says the girl so determined that no one loves
her that she'll make it so!" Colin exclaimed.

She scowled at him. "You don't understand.
If I go to school, they won't like me like you do.
I'll go back to being alone as I used to be, and I
don't think I can bear that." Her voice rose. "I like
it here too much. I like this"—she swept her arm
around—"and both of you."

Hector interrupted them by barking frantically. Mary frowned. What was he doing?

They all turned. In the distance, from the

direction of the house, they could see smoke rising into the sky. "That smoke," said Colin, his expression turning to alarm. "Is that normal?"

"No," said Dickon anxiously.

"It's coming from the house! There must be a fire!" gasped Mary.

"Father!" Colin cried.

"Martha!" said Dickon, in fear.

Mary didn't hesitate. She sprinted toward the gate. Dickon followed. Colin took a few hobbling steps after them. Mary glanced back and saw the frustration and defeat in his face.

"I can't!" he shouted. "But you go . . . GO!"

21
The Fire

Mary and Dickon raced toward the house. There were flames at every window and black smoke billowing up into the blue sky. The house was burning to the ground!

As they reached the front door, Martha staggered out, coughing and spluttering. "Mary! Dickon! Stay away. The brigade's been called. We can't do anything more."

"Is everyone out?" demanded Mary.

"Not the master," said Martha, her eyes filling with tears. "We don't know where he is. No one's seen him since the blaze started."

Mary sprinted toward the door, leaping up the steps.

"Mary!" Dickon shouted.

"I know where he'll be!" Mary yelled. She raced across the hall and up the stairs. The air was smotheringly hot, smoke billowing down the staircase, making her eyes stream. The house was filled with the crackling of fire and crashes of objects as the hungry flames devoured them. Mary ran up to the second floor and raced to Colin's room. The door was open, and her uncle was standing inside, looking around helplessly as if he didn't know what to do.

"I knew you'd be here," Mary gasped.

Her uncle shook as he coughed. His face was smudged with dirt, his hair in disarray. "Colin, where's Colin?" he gasped as the fire raged through the house.

"Come on, please, come on," Mary said, tugging his arm.

"I will not leave without my son!" her uncle said, shaking his head. "I can't desert him. Not again."

"Your son isn't here, sir," insisted Mary.

Her uncle's face creased with grief. "He is dead already?"

"No! I was with him just five minutes ago. I give you my word on the soul of Grace Craven. Now please, come with me and I will show you where he is!" Mary knew she had to get him out quickly. She tugged his arm again, and this time he allowed her to pull him out of the room as the flames began to engulf it. His face was dazed.

Mary pulled him down the smoke-filled corridor, but as they reached the stairs there was a crack overhead and part of the ceiling fell down, the plaster burning. Mary yelped and jumped back. The house was burning down around them. "We need to find another way."

She turned and led him past Colin's room, but as they hurried through the smoke, the floor in front of them gave way, flames leaping up through it.

We're trapped, thought Mary in despair. *We're going to be burned alive.* She turned to her uncle. "Uncle, you know the house best. How can we get out?"

Coughing hard, her uncle collapsed on the floor.

"No!" she cried in dismay. "Please don't—I can't lift you." She tried to drag him back to his feet, but he shook his head.

"Leave me. Please. Leave me here," he said in despair.

Mary shook her head stubbornly. "No. Colin needs you."

"I've ruined everything," her uncle croaked.

Mary heard footsteps. Looking up, she saw the ghostly figures of her mother and Aunt Grace appear in the corridor. Her eyes met theirs—pleading, begging. In an instant, Grace was beside her, her hands helping her uncle to his feet. Then she was gone again, running to join her sister by the door that led to the hidden room. They both looked straight at Mary.

Mary was sure they were trying to help. "This way!" she gasped.

Mary helped her uncle along the corridor, following the ghostly figures. Her mother and Grace went into the room with the murals and disappeared through the wall into the secret room. Mary pressed the hidden catch and desperately pushed her uncle into the room, slamming the door behind them. The sisters were standing on the far side of the room. With a conspiratorial look, they suddenly vanished.

"No!" Mary cried. And then she saw it. Another door right where they had been standing. It was small and thin, disguised by the wallpaper, but it had a little round handle. Mary turned the handle, but the door was locked.

"Uncle, help me!" she cried, starting to kick at the flimsy door. She looked back at him. He was kneeling on the floor again, looking around at all the dresses, tears in his eyes. "I need your help!"

He staggered to his feet and ran at the door with all his weight. It splintered and gave way, and they fell through into a servants' staircase. It was free from fire. They stumbled down it and came out through a door onto the main staircase of the hall. Flames were licking at the stairs. The figures of her mother and Grace appeared in front of them, running down toward the hall. Mary grabbed her uncle's hand and followed them. As they neared the bottom, smoke billowed up from the stairwell. Mr. Craven lost his footing and fell, dragging Mary with him. Together they crashed to the bottom, landing in a heap on the tiled floor of the entrance hall.

For a moment, Mary was too dazed to move. She looked up woozily and saw her mother bending over her. "Mother?" She wasn't sure if she thought it or spoke it out loud, but her mother smiled.

"Oh, Mother, I've ruined everything," Mary said, tears filling her eyes. "And I just wanted to make things better."

Her mother reached out and stroked her cheek.

Mary's heart stopped still. "Please stay," she begged.

Her mother gave a sad shake of her head and kissed Mary's hair. At the ghostly touch of her lips, Mary felt the deep surge of her mother's love. Their eyes met one last time, then Mary's mother smiled tenderly and was gone.

"Mary!" she heard Dickon yell, and he and Martha came charging through the smoke, coughing. "Mary, are you—"

"Get my uncle!" she screamed. "Take him first!"

Martha and Dickon lifted Mr. Craven up by the arms. Dickon looked around to help Mary too, but she was already struggling to her feet. As she reached the door, she glanced back and saw the smiling figures of her mother and Grace standing at the foot of the grand staircase. Their faces were happy and peaceful. Taking hold of each other's hands, they walked upstairs into the flames, reclaiming their home and vanishing from sight.

Goodbye, Mary thought.

Coughing and gasping for breath, she staggered out of the door and into the fresh air.

22

Believe in Magic

Martha and Dickon pulled Mary away from
the house. She collapsed next to her uncle,
drawing in deep breaths. Her uncle's clothes and
face were covered in soot and ash, and she knew
she looked no better.

"Room! Give them room!" cried Mrs. Medlock, flapping around them as the sound of sirens
and the fire brigade arrived.

"What were you thinking, girl? That was very, very stupid of you," Mrs. Pitcher scolded Mary, not looking like she knew whether to laugh or cry.

"And very brave," said Martha, helping Mary to sit up.

Mary met Dickon's worried eyes and felt a rush of relief. She'd done it. She'd saved her uncle.

Mr. Craven struggled to his feet. He looked like a broken man. "Show me," he said hoarsely to Mary. "Show me my son. I must see him."

Mary looked at Dickon, who gave a small nod.

"It's this way, sir," Mary said to her uncle.

She and Dickon led the way to the ivy-covered gate. Mary glanced at her uncle and saw that his face was rigid. "Colin's in here," she said, pushing back the creepers and turning the gate's handle.

As her uncle and Mrs. Medlock stepped into the garden, the sun shone down through the long canopy of yellow laburnum flowers. Mary saw the astonishment on her uncle's and Mrs. Medlock's faces as they walked through the beautiful golden tunnel and out into the garden with its formal flower beds bursting with blooms.

"Why, it's beautiful!" Mrs. Medlock said wonderingly as she looked around at the overflowing flower beds, the tended trees, and the gravel path that was now free from weeds.

"It's ours," said Mary. She glanced at her uncle, who was staring around in shock at the blooming garden with its riot of flowers. "It was hers, but now I think she wants us to share it."

"And he's here?" Her uncle looked at her pleadingly. "Where is my son?"

"Call for him, sir," said Mary encouragingly.

Her uncle moved swiftly through the garden. "Colin?" he called, pushing plants aside as he searched. "Colin?" Mary, Dickon, and Mrs. Medlock followed.

"Please be careful, sir," said Mrs. Medlock anxiously, but Mr. Craven ignored her.

"Colin!" His voice rose.

Colin was sitting on the grass by the temple, his sleeves rolled up. "There!" Mary said, pulling her uncle's sleeve and pointing.

"Father!" Colin shouted in relief. "You're safe!"

Mr. Craven broke into an unsteady run. Mary bounded beside him. He stopped a little way from Colin and stared as if he couldn't believe his eyes. "I thought I'd lost you," he whispered, his eyes riveted on his son's face. "And of all the places to find you. Here. In her garden . . ."

He stepped closer, but Colin shook his head. "No, wait. Please, Father." He began to struggle to his knees and, using a stick that Dickon had carved for him, he pulled himself to his feet. He smiled proudly at his father.

Mr. Craven paled. "You are standing, Colin!"

Colin nodded and took a step toward his father.

He paused, then took another and another. Mr. Craven watched, transfixed. "But how is this possible?" he whispered.

Colin stumbled the last few steps and fell forward into his father's arms. "Magic," he said as his father grabbed him. Their eyes met. "Secrets." He glanced around the garden. *"Her."*

"Her?" said his father, confused.

"His mother," said Mary.

Mrs. Medlock spoke. "She's here. I'm sure of it, sir," she said, and her voice was warmer than Mary had ever heard it before. She and Mr. Craven looked at each other over Colin's head and a tear fell down Mr. Craven's cheek. With a groan, he hugged Colin as if he would never let him go. Eventually, he pulled back.

"Forgive me, Colin. I should have visited you more, and then I would have realized you did not need the medicine. But it was . . ." He swallowed. "Too hard for me. I am sorry, so very sorry."

"It's all right, Father," Colin said, his eyes bright with tears. "I understand. You have been in a prison as much as I."

His father looked at him wonderingly. "How is it that we are taught by our children?"

Mary exchanged looks with Dickon. *We have all taught each other,* she thought. *And the garden had taught us most of all.*

Colin's voice became brisk. "Enough of this. Tell me, Father. How do you like our garden? Would you like me to give you the grand tour?"

A smile lit up his father's face. "Yes, Colin," he said, clearing his throat and nodding. "I believe I would like that very much."

With a grin, Colin began to hobble around the garden, pointing out the different plants to his father and Mrs. Medlock. Mary smiled at Dickon as they followed on behind, with Hector trotting at their heels.

23

Four Months Later . . .

Mary, Colin, and Dickon sat on the bank of the stream, dangling their legs in the clear water while Hector nosed in the bushes beside them. Spring had passed, and the garden was a riot of summer flowers—tall hollyhocks and Canterbury bells, scrambling roses, twining sweet peas and honeysuckle, beds of lilac lavender and pink geraniums and joyful bright yellow and red dahlias. The gate to the garden stood open all the time, and the house was a very different place. Mary's uncle had dedicated himself to rebuilding it, opening up the old rooms, organizing the builders and decorators, his soul coming to life again as he constructed a new home from the ashes of a prison. The plan to send Mary away to school had been dropped on the day of the fire, and now Mr. Craven used the books in his library to teach Colin and Mary about the world.

He had employed more staff so Mrs. Medlock, Martha, and Mrs. Pitcher didn't have to work so hard, and the house was a bustling, happy place again. Dickon was now the official gardener. He could still slip through the mist like a shadow but was more often to be seen strolling through the grounds, whistling, with Hector at his heels.

After their morning lessons were over, Colin and Mary always fetched their lunch from Mrs.

Pitcher—with extra Spam for Hector—and met up with Dickon and Hector in the secret garden. They spent their afternoons together, taking care of it, weeding, separating out plants that were too close to each other. They would also play, and Mary would tell them all stories. Their laughter seemed to make the plants grow, and every day Colin became stronger and healthier. He could run now—and swim and dive.

"Tell us a story, Mary," he said as they splashed the water with their toes.

"Very well." Mary looked at her two best friends and felt happiness fill her. "There were once three people who loved each other very much. . . ." she began.

"Four," interrupted Colin, putting his arm around Hector. "What about Hector?"

"Maybe I was including Hector and not you," Mary teased.

Colin picked a handful of grass and threw it at her. "I want there to be five people in this story—no six—Hector, my father, and Martha too."

Dickon nodded. "Yes, put Martha in."

"If you both don't pipe down, I shan't tell the story at all!" Mary said tartly.

The boys exchanged looks. "Sorry, Mary," they said together.

"Thank you." She settled herself into a more comfortable position. "Now, if you are ready and silent, I shall try again." She gave them an impish grin. "There were once *some* people who lived in an old deserted house together. And they had a garden of their own—a secret garden that they discovered."

The robin perched on a nearby rock. It twittered at her encouragingly, and she smiled.

"There were friendly birds and animals in the garden, a healing stream, and loving ghosts who watched over it," she continued. "The people who lived there didn't know it at first, but it was a magic garden and the more they visited the garden, the stronger and healthier they grew."

Colin nodded with satisfaction.

"They were all happy together—very happy." Mary looked around. The air of the garden seemed to sparkle with secrets that had been imprisoned but had now been told. Joy filled her. "The people saved the garden as much as it saved them," she said softly. "Because they believed in its magic."

A wind rustled through the flowers and trees.

"*Magic,*" the garden whispered back.